Advance Praise for Hoeism: Born To Do It

"You will enjoy every word of English Ruler's vividly compelling and highly entertaining debut novel. 'HOEISM' is an instant classic!" National Best Selling Author ~Julia Press Simmons

"It's that time of year, when book stores clogs with novels trying to finish the year strong with a great fourth quarter. HOEISM is undoubtedly a leader of the pact."~Rahiem Brooks

HOEISM

Born To Do It

English Ruler

Acknowledgements

First and foremost I'd like to thank the Almighty for giving me the power and strength to complete this project.

To my family, in particular, Liv, Olivia, and Livi Elijah: Thanks for always being there to support and push me when I needed a motivational boost. Your presence in my life has caused me to challenge myself and settle for nothing less than the best. Knowing that your love and comfort will always be awaiting me makes each tribulation, no matter how great, a worthy one.

There are a few people who have shamelessly extended themselves to the successful completion of this book by offering assistance, advice, encouragement, connections, time, and in some cases, just a listening ear;

Loretta R Walls aka "The Princess of Urban Fiction," there are no words to express my gratitude for taking me under your wing. Your constant pep talks, early morning phone calls, and friendship helped keep me focused, especially toward the end. Whenever I thought it wouldn't get completed, you were there to offer a perspective that was hard to ignore. You are as real as it gets, and I'm glad to know you.

Rahiem "The Authortainer" Brooks: Thanks for always approaching things from a business perspective and allowing me to see the potential when one stays focused and educated on the market. You have always been generous with your knowledge and that is to be commended. I truly appreciate all of your help.

Chantel Richards: You were the very first person to read the story and my very first supporter. Thanks for your encouragement. It's finally show time!

Yoshe: Seems like years since I was discussing this all with you, and look where we are now. Thanks for the phone calls and advice.

Kamilah N. Watson: Your boy Lowell is making his appearance! We go back a long time 'Milah, so it's especially sweet that you were such an integral part of this. Your calls each time you read a snippet were one of the things that kept me driven.

Moody Holiday: Without request, you took time out of your busy schedule to provide an honest critique that I cannot put a value on. You taught me a lot, and I thank you for it.

Christine & Dominique Gordon: Thanks for lending yourself to my cause at such short notice. Although things didn't come together as originally planned, the end result is "da bomb" and I have both of you to thank for it.

Envy Red: You have helped me more than you even know and unwittingly gave me the fire I needed to continue past a few hundred words. For that you have my unwavering gratitude.

LL the Story Tailor: Thanks for the snip and tuck. Your attention to detail is to be commended.

Gregory Graphics: Thanks for the hot cover. It was great working with you. You captured the essence of my vision and created a cover image that is hard to ignore.

To my first "Hoeism Reading Crew!!": Towanta Jones, Rudolph Edwards, Tanya "Bigga T" Kerr, Karen Z, Maxine Block aka "The REAL Maxine" and Marissa McGhee thanks for cursing me out, kissing your teeth, and getting an attitude after taking the time to read snippets. Your emotion let me know I was on the right path. I'm happy to finally present you with the finished product. Maxine...when you're done you should know the two words I want to hear - DAMN GINA!

Sometimes people provide something valuable like a strong presence, kind words, or just a random phone call or email that puts you where you need to be for the moment. These people have provided motivation and strength just by being their kind-hearted selves: Clarissa "Lighthouse" Johnson, Carmen Blalock aka Miss C Solo, Treasure Blue, Trae Ferguson, D. Lynn Blalock, Chris Mainor, and Felisha Bradshaw.

To My Friends: Julie Nin, Nelson Nin, Julia Press-Simmons, K'wan Foye, Iris Bolling, June Miller, Rickey Teems, Karen E. Quinones Miller, Arlene Brathwaite, Ali Brathwaite, Steven Van Patten, Denise Rosier and Norma Vandemark. Thanks for your continued support.

To The Ladies of ARC: Locksie, SiStar Tea, Shai, Delonya, and S'mone you all are always there to help and offer advice, a laugh, a hug, a lashing - whatever...and I can't thank you enough. You're more than friends, you're family.

Shout Outs: Orsayor Simmons, Fabiola Joseph, Trae Ferguson, The1Essence, Urban Reviews, Grace Nails (Mt. Vernon, NY), 111 Deli (Hauppauge, NY), Urban Grapevine Magazine, ARC FB Group, Liz Ramos, Janet Cintron, Ann Lyons, DeeWorks Live, Julie Ann Ryan of London's Colourful Radio, Nu Cherte Publishing, Siri Enterprises and Universal Write Publishing, Heather DeClemente, and Bruce Towell.

HOEISM: *To possess the characteristics and act in ways that are hoe, tramp, hooker, prostitute, skank, and/or slut-like.*

Prologue

Shanae had a feeling something was up as Tremaine whipped the Altima LS around a sharp corner, causing her body to slide and press up intimately against the passenger-side door. She knew her man and he was not an aggressive driver.

The way his strong, well-manicured hands gripped the steering wheel as he mastered another sharp maneuver made her study him a little more closely. His jaw was clenched tightly and he shot her a menacing glance before looking away and shaking his head. He picked her up from work on time for a change. However, despite the warm greeting she gave upon her entry into the vehicle, Tremaine offered no more than a cocky head nod.

Every attempt she made to initiate conversation went ignored. She looked him up and down, from his crisp baby blue golf shirt and snug silk slacks, to his freshly polished Aldo loafers manipulating the pedals. She brought her focus back up and tried to bore a hole into the side of his head with her eyes hoping that would yield some form of reaction.

Nothing.

Being the upfront kind of woman she was, Shanae decided to nip shit in the bud. "Trey, what's up with the silent treatment?" She turned to face him when he suddenly jammed on the breaks to heed the red light before them. A few of her cosmetics escaped her knock off Coach bag when it crashed to the floor in response.

Screwing up his face, Tremaine looked her up and down, "You really wanna know? I can show you better than I can tell you," he stated, turning around to give her his profile once again.

Shanae retrieved her fallen items, lifted her hands and dropped them in her lap, resigned. She was truly baffled. She had a pretty good relationship with Tremaine for the last year and a half. Despite the usual squabbles couples go through, they'd never had a real argument. The tension was driving her insane as she watched the scenery of Lower Westchester, NY whisk by. As they passed Provost Avenue, she grew even more concerned.

"Trey, what the fuck's going on? You just passed our turn."

Tremaine remained quiet, never taking his eyes off the road. Shanae decided to chill until he decided to reveal what was on his mind. The stress of a busy workday seemed to take up residence in the crevices of her neck and she rolled her head around in an attempt to provide some relief to the stiffness. Fuck it! I ain't got time for this bitchassness! She sat back, closed her eyes, and massaged her temples wondering how much longer her car would be held hostage at the mechanic.

Tremaine felt like a fool. Never in his life had he allowed a female to clown him. He was that nigga! His six feet two inches tall frame boasted broad shoulders, milk chocolate skin, a squeezable ass, and nice teeth. Having his own vehicle, a prosperous career and his own residence –solidified this full package. There was no reason to settle for less or get suckered into some bullshit. Yet still, here he was. It was his fault, really. Shanae's cocked bottom, thick thighs, and succulent lips won him over before he even knew her name. Once he got to know her, he realized that even though she was a little ghetto, she wasn't a dumb broad. A bit hood, but her rough edges could be smoothed out.   It was with this mentality that he embarked on a relationship with her.

Shanae dragging her feet because the truth of the matter was that he knew how this was going to play out while she could only hope and pray for the best.

They arrived at the receptionist desk and Shanae gave her name. The older lady behind the partition instructed her to sign in and wait for her name to be called. As they took seats in the waiting area, Tremaine surveyed the females around him. The women were a mixture of ages and races. I wonder if these bitches is as trifling as Shanae. How many of their men don't know what they skank asses is up to?!

Shanae, on the other hand, was nerve wracked. She didn't want to believe her secret had been found out, but she was trying to mentally prepare herself for the worst. The reality of the situation was that she had no back-up plan, so there was only but so much preparation she could do.

"Shanae Alexander?" called a pencil-thin blonde donning a white lab coat. Shanae stood up and Tremaine followed. They were directed into a small examination room.

"So how are you feeling today?" asked the nurse who introduced herself as Karen.

"Pretty good," Shanae responded. She was shaking her leg like a child about to get a spanking, as she needed an outlet for her nervousness.

"Have you had any severe cramping? And are you bleeding at the moment?" Karen continued as she referred to the clipboard in front of her.

Shanae just wanted to disappear, "No, and no."

Karen jotted down some notes and turned back to Shanae, "Okay, we're going to perform a pap-smear and then discuss your options for birth control to prevent anymore unwanted pregnancies. Do you have any questions?"

Shanae could only shake her head and look at the ground. The cat was out the bag. Tremaine could not believe his ears. It was one thing to know the fact, but when spoken, it just put things into a whole new perspective.

"I have a question," he voiced. "Could you refresh me on how far along the pregnancy was?" Tremaine was no fool and wanted to rub Shanae's face in the shitty diaper she created. He wanted to punk her as she did him.

Karen, aware of the couples' strange behavior, glanced over at Shanae for approval. Shanae turned to Tremaine, "Nine weeks," she stated boldly.

Karen sensed the couple needed a moment alone. "Well, I'm going to give you a moment to undress for the examination," she informed Shanae. Turning to Tremaine she said, "When I get back I'm gonna have to ask you to step out so we can do the check-up."

Tremaine nodded his head. The nurse's departure created even greater tension in the room. He was the first to speak, "You still wanna ask me what my problem is?"

Shanae looked up at him to see a thick vein throbbing on the side of his head. She parted her lips to speak but no words came out.

"You're a dirty half cent hoe if I ever saw one," said Tremaine nastily. He figured now would be a better time than any to give her the envelope. Shanae was more interested in what he was pulling out of his back pant pocket more than the insulting words he directed her way. She knew he spoke the truth. With dramatic flair, Tremaine unfolded the contents of the manila envelope. He looked them over, shook his head and handed them to Shanae who swore she saw moisture in his eyes. "Next time you wanna to play games do it with someone who lacks as much common intelligence as you do." With that, he exited the local clinic without a backward glance.

It was no secret that Tremaine would never be able to father a child due to injuries sustained in a childhood accident, but the devastation Shanae brought to a man that truly loved her meant nothing. She was too calculating to be concerned with Tremaine and his sterile ass! She just knew she was lucky that her excuse of taking birth control to regulate her period lasted this long. The truth was quite obvious now.   Sitting alone in the chilly examination room, the only thoughts that occupied Shanae's mind were how to rectify the situation with the person who wrote the letter in her hands. This bastard was more cold-hearted than she was by far. Now that's saying something...

Chapter 1

It was almost 6:30p.m. and Giselle Frasier was no closer to putting dinner on the table than when she walked in the door an hour ago. This April 15th found her job as a tax preparer especially challenging. She was completely spent after a long day of punching numbers and printing forms. It was as if her clients felt as though she should be overly accommodating because they waited until the last minute to handle their business. Today was the day that she received the cut eyes, deep sighs and obvious time checking, as if to say, "Bitch, it's the last day before penalties, you betta hurry yo' ass up."

I'm sorry you're stupid ass waited until the deadline to do what you knew had to be done ages ago. Now I'm supposed to be the one jumping up and down to help put money in your pocket. Fuck outta here! Now, Giselle was glad to be in the comfort of her own home, but her kids had her seriously pondering if home should still be looked at as a place of refuge.

Marcelle had the kitchen littered with various items and ingredients to be used in his science project, and Nicola had three friends in the living room mimicking the dance moves to Beyonce's 'Run The World' video. All Giselle wanted to do was relax and wind down, but the laughter, music and stomping coming from the living room coupled with the mess and confusion of the kitchen grated her nerves. Her plan was to prepare a quick meal of chicken parmesan with spaghetti before jumping into a hot shower, but with Marcelle playing 'weird scientist' there was gonna have to be a change in plans. She was just about to address the issues in the kitchen when the front door swung open.

Lowell Washington walked into his home and was greeted by the chant, "Who run the world? Girls! (Girls!)" and eight feet marching and tapping on the hard wood floor. Oh boy, he thought, as he maneuvered his way to the bottom of the staircase.

"Hi Mr. Washington," the girls shouted out in unison.

"Hey Low," shouted Nicola as she mimicked the dance moves.

"Good evening ladies, I see you all are getting your workout." Lowell took a few steps up and then paused to converse with the girls. They laughed.

Jadaine commented, "It wasn't supposed to be this hard, but we don't have Bey's choreographer."

Nicola swatted her friend with a throw pillow. "And it'll never be easy for you if you don't stay focused." She was no fool. She knew her friend had a school girl crush on her stepdad.

Lowell's chocolate covered skin covered 6' 4", 210 pounds of lean, taut muscle. Close cropped hair covered his head, and he sported a neatly trimmed goatee that enhanced his full lips. His left ear displayed a diamond encrusted bezel and a tiny but noticeable scar was just above his right eyebrow, adding an air of roughness to his image. He was a looker and Nicola couldn't blame Jadaine for pushing up. Lowell had been in her life for six years and Nicola loved him like a real dad. Though her biological father was present in her life, she had this unspoken connection with Lowell.

"Where's your mom?" asked Lowell, ascending the steps.

"I think she's in the kitchen."

"Okay," he called out as he reached the second floor landing. He went into the bedroom he shared with Giselle, changed his clothes and returned to the first floor in sweats and a t-shirt. Giselle was tending to a pot on the stove while Marcelle was wiping down the countertop as Lowell entered the kitchen.

Marcelle walked over and exchanged pounds with Lowell. At eight-years-old, he was trying to emulate the males in his life and exhibit more mature behavior.

"What's cooking, love?" Lowell walked up behind Giselle and wrapped his arm around her waist.

He inhaled her Dolce & Gabbana Light Blue fragrance as he held her close.

Giselle greeted him with a peck on the lips, "Nothing much, just tryna get this place in order and put some food together so we can eat. You see that child in there with her dance troupe?" She laughed.

"Yeah I saw them," Lowell shook his head. A half smile appeared as he thought about the child he helped raise for almost half of her life. Although he loved both of Giselle's children, he had a soft spot for Nicola. She could do no wrong in his eyes.

Lowell turned his attention to Marcelle who was now rinsing out a plastic pitcher. "So what are you doing in the kitchen, we all know you don't clean."

"Whatever! I have a science project and I was trying to figure out what experiment to do," Marcelle explained.

Giselle spun around, "You mean you created all that mess and you don't even know what you're doing?" She was annoyed.

Marcelle shrugged, "I narrowed it down."

Lowell saw Giselle's brown eyes flicker and knew she was about to lay into her son. He took steps to diffuse the situation. "Babe, why don't you go upstairs and relax a bit? I'll finish up down here."

Giselle was thankful for the offer. Heading upstairs, she thought about how lucky she was to have Lowell in her life. He was a good provider, had a decent job, and most importantly, he was good with her children. His top of the line bedroom skills were an added bonus. Giselle was looking forward to becoming Mrs. Washington, although Lowell had never asked. They did have conversations on the matter, but they never went any further than that. She hoped they would make it official one day soon.

At thirty-two, she was ready to have one more child and get on with her life, but after too many failed relationships under her belt, she wanted to solidify things with marriage first. Lowell was two years younger and had no kids of his own. Since he was such a great male figure for her kids, she was certain a child they created together would round out their family unit. However, without walking down the aisle, she would not be allowing his sperm to christen any of her eggs.

Half an hour later Nicola's company had made their exit, and order was restored in the household. The family discussed summer vacation choices over dinner at the dining room table.

"What about Jamaica? We haven't done the tourist thing over there yet. Daddy just takes us to all the local places and to visit family. I wanna see the places I see on TV," Nicola stated.

Giselle saw Nicola's point. Being a Jamaican native, her ex, Patrick, enjoyed taking the kids to the local joints as opposed to the more appealing tourist attractions. Before she could offer an opinion, Marcelle chimed in.

"Man, forget Jamaica. Let's go to Puerto Rico, Ma. I can come back and be the new Pitbull, Dale!" Everyone laughed. Marcelle was a true joker.

"I was thinking we could do a cruise, that way we could visit more than one place," Giselle said between bites. She looked forward to the yearly excursions they took together.

Lowell loved the sound of that, "That sounds good, what ports were you thinking of?"

"Well Carnival has a six day Caribbean cruise leaving from Fort Lauderdale with stops at Key West, the Cayman Islands, and Jamaica," Giselle answered

"YEAH BABAAY!" Nicola was all for it, "Can we go, Mom? That sounds too cool."

Nicola was all gung ho once she heard Jamaica. All she wanted to do was finally learn how to do the new "cow foot" dance and try to meet Reggae entertainer Vybez Cartel. Giselle turned to Marcelle with questioning eyes.

"Sounds good to me," he was just excited to be going on a big ship.

That left Lowell. With all eyes on him, Lowell decided to have some fun. He stroked his chin and looked up in the air, "Well I'm not sure my delicate skin can take the heat of the hot Jamaican sun, and I don't wanna give any retired old lady a heart attack in

Ft. Lauderdale with my buff, sculpted physique, and last but not least, Cayman Islands…do ya'll really wanna go there? Sounds like Cave Man Island, I'm just sayin'!"

Collectively they tried to keep in their laughs, but Marcelle was the first one to crack. He erupted in a fit of giggles and everyone followed suit, including Lowell.

"For real though, that sounds like a plan. Go 'head and book it Giselle, it'll give us something to look forward to. We have a full staff at the plant so there should be no problem with me taking the usual time off."

"Okay," was Giselle's reply.

Lowell stood up to take his plate to the sink and stumbled. His glass crashed to the floor. "Damn!"

"You all right, Lowe?" Giselle asked, concerned as she rose out of her seat.

"I'm fine. My foot fell asleep…I can barely feel it," Lowell took a seat back at the table.

"That's been happening to you a lot lately. And the other day it was your hand," she said with concern in her voice as she swept up the broken glass.

"Nah, it's just once in a while," he quipped.

"No, this is the third or fourth time this week that you've had severe numbing of your hands or feet. You shouldn't be ignoring this." She felt that something wasn't right. Men in general hate to go to the doctor, so she knew it would be a fight to get him to make an appointment.

Lowell was trying his best to downplay the incident. He knew something was wrong, but he didn't want to face any bad news. He was glad that he'd been able to hide this situation with the numbness as long as he had. No way was he going to tell her about his blurry vision spells. Lowell's recent health issues were becoming harder to hide, much less ignore. Sooner than later, he was going to have to face the music.

Chapter 2

Timothy Starks sat in his six by eight foot cubicle at American Motor Products Services preparing to start his work day. When prompted for his password, he tapped the appropriate buttons on the keyboard, and then waited for the computer monitor to display his personalized JETS logo desktop. He rotated his office chair side to side, as he anticipated the arrival of his co-worker and office neighbor.

Thinking about her healthy thighs and sexy strut brought stiffness to his manhood. He shifted in his seat and reached into his pant pocket to retrieve his iPhone. Accessing the camera application, he pulled up a photo that never ceased to make him salivate. His co-worker's shapely legs were encased in a pair of shiny black leggings as she bent over to access her file cabinet. The fitted royal blue sweater she wore gave the illusion of a mini dress as it barely covered her rotund backside. He snapped the picture a few weeks ago when she wasn't looking; one of many candid photos of her he had secretly collected. This type of behavior was normal for Timothy. He was a pervert in every sense of the word. His even-toned dark skin and solid physique got him noticed by the ladies; it was hard for them to resist such a fine specimen. However, his callous ways and nasty demeanor were immediate deal breakers.

Within minutes of meeting a female, Timothy would shoot off at the mouth with some crude comment or another. It just came natural for him. Women scorned him and men disparaged him. He seemed to be some sort of human conundrum. People were often surprised to find out he was married, however, anyone close enough to know the truth just felt sorry for his wife. Eight years of marriage, over six years of verbal and physical abuse, and the stripping of her self-esteem had not prompted Penny Starks to file for divorce. It was anyone's guess why she stayed. The couple had no children, so one could only assume that she endured his manic behavior because she didn't think she deserved better. Penny was well aware of Timothy's affairs; he made no effort to hide them.

He pushed the envelope when it came to his abusive treatment of women, and the workplace was no different. Working for a small private company like AMP Services made it easy for him to get away with this type of misconduct. Almost everyone at AMP had been there several years, and no one wanted to ruffle any feathers. It was a matter of sticking to the evils that you know. That's the problem with getting comfortable, there's little hope for change.

HOEISM: BORNTODOIT

In an office with a ninety-five percent female population, Timothy was in his glory. Being reprimanded was a long shot. He was a menace to the women in the office. They were all aware of his character and tried to avoid him at all costs. Although he didn't discriminate, he took a special interest in harassing this one woman that sat behind him. He got his chance to take his inappropriate behavior to the next level when he caught her attempting to steal company property.

For fear of losing her job, she let him smash her occasionally. Yet Timothy was ready for more than the occasional fuck. He wanted to live out the fantasies in his sick mind, and that entailed getting in her panties more often than the few times he already had.

He was concerned that she hadn't been to work in a few days. The corners of his mouth turned up and a wide smile spread across his face when he thought that maybe his recent antics finally put her in her place. She had tried to end their sick affair, but he pulled his trump card. Maybe now she'd know he was not one to be fucked with, figuratively speaking of course!

One week had passed since Shanae's secret abortion was revealed at the clinic. Tremaine had demanded that she leave his apartment immediately and she obliged. Since she had nowhere to go once

Tremaine threw her out, most of her belongings were housed at a local Public Storage facility. With no friends or family to put her up, she was forced to accept an illegal room in a boarding house.

Shanae had no real friends, which was not uncommon for a girl with loose tendencies, such as herself. Those types of women usually don't trust females because they know in their heart they themselves can't be trusted – so how can they put trust in anyone? It's the simple case of 'I know I would do it, so they would too.'

Melanie, Shanae's older sister, would have taken her in; at least until she found an apartment, but Shanae's pride wouldn't allow her to go. It was already bad enough that she had to share that her indiscretions was the reason for the end of her relationship. No way did she want to be around the success of her sister while she was at one of the lowest points in her life.

Although Melanie and Shanae had a good relationship, Shanae always felt overshadowed by her sister. A happily married physical therapist with one daughter, Melanie was successful and lived comfortably. She owned her own home, vehicle, and was able to take her family on trips whenever she desired. This was a sharp contrast to the paycheck-to-paycheck life that Shanae was accustomed to. Entry-level customer service left much to be desired, but it provided employment, for which Shanae was grateful.

With Tremaine's income no longer available to fall back on, Shanae was forced to return to work after using a few of her last vacation days to adjust her living situation. She pulled into her office building's parking lot and found a spot close to the entrance. After checking her make-up in the rearview mirror, she made her way inside, stopping to chat with a few co-workers on the way.

Approaching her desk, Shanae saw the message indicator blinking and dreaded the multitude of messages that awaited her. At her work station, she clocked in and booted up her computer. She then closed her eyes and said a silent prayer for the day to go well. Shanae had avoided confronting the author of the letter that was sent to Tremaine because she knew it would open up the door for even more complex issues, and she just wasn't ready to deal with them. It had come down to the wire and today she was forced to face the music. She didn't have any tangible proof that 'he' was the one who wrote it, but the hints that were dropped in the letter spoke volumes.

I feel sorry for you man. She's mad triflin'… you have no idea. Most nights she goes home to you, she's already had her back worn out so I know she can't be giving it to you that good. Oh yeah before I forget, congratulations! I've heard that she's expecting. An abortion that is! Bitch got Planned Parenthood on speed dial. It's probably for the better anyway 'cause I sure as hell ain't ready for no baby mama drama – plus I wore like two condoms every time we smashed. And the way she talks about you she don't love you no way. If she did, she wouldn't make it so easy for me to hit it day in and day out. Plus, she be snappin' on you and your weak sperm on the regular. She knew what she was doin'. Only a dumb bitch goes puttin' her man down to another, makes it easy as hell for that man to get the draws. Victoria's Secret my ass! Even Victoria's talkin' about this bitch's nasty ways. Yeah, the pussy has gotten around, but it's still good. And as long as she gives it – I'ma take it. It was easy to get, you know she a hoe anyway. I'ma keep hittin' it, I just want you to know 'cause I ain't easin' up. She wanna keep shit on the low, but I don't have time for the games. We all adults here, I ain't got no problems with you, but know that the pussy is as much every other mans as it is yours. Don't get it twisted just because you tryna wife the bitch!

Shanae let out an exaggerated sigh and shook her head as she put on her headset and prepared to take her first call of the day. She had to get back into the groove of things and get past this hump.

Busy fielding calls all morning, Shanae tried her best to concentrate, but she felt as though she was being watched. Better yet, she knew it. Lunchtime would be anything but peaceful today. This man was determined to bring her down and she was not going to let him succeed. Although it was stupid, her poor decision to steal two high-powered vacuum cleaners from the job was the catalyst for the sad situation she was in now. Timothy thought he was slick sending Tremaine a letter…fuck him. Let me deal with this ass 'cause this shit got to stop.

Twelve o'clock rolled around and before Shanae could get her things together, Maxine from the accounting department appeared at her desk, "You wanna grab a bite to eat? Seems like forever since we did lunch." Maxine was a cool ass white chick, and one of the few people at AMP whom Shanae really got along with. She and Shanae had become rather close during their employment at the motor parts company. It was a running joke that she should have been black given the way she behaved, not to mention her name.

Shanae looked at her and frowned, "Max, how are you? I'd love to but I have a few errands to run, how about Friday?"

"Fridays cool, don't flake on me though," Maxine pointed a finger at Shanae to stress her last statement.

Shanae smiled at her as she walked away, "I got you, chica."

As if on cue, Timothy stood and peered at Shanae over the cubicle partition. "I think we have some unfinished business, Shan." The lust in his eyes made her skin crawl. The smile on Shanae's lips slowly dissipated as she took in the man before her.

"I don't know about that, but I do need to speak with you."

"Whatever, lets bounce," Timothy said and headed toward the exit, diddy boppin' just a bit.

Shanae grabbed her purse and followed him out of the building, her short sundress flowing in the wind with each step. Maxine viewed the exchange from her desk across the office. She didn't trust Timothy as far as she could throw him. Something about the exchange between the couple didn't sit right with her. She'd be talking to Shanae about this…

May was fast approaching and the weather was a pleasant 75 degrees in New Rochelle, NY. To avoid the prying eyes of AMP employees, Shanae and Timothy decided to drive out to Hudson Park, which was a short distance away from the office. The drive over was a silent one, each wrapped up in their own thoughts.

Shanae was hoping things with Timothy were over now that he went out of his way to destroy her relationship with Tremaine.

Timothy's thought process was on the other side of the spectrum; he was contemplating how he could keep Shanae under his thumb as long as possible. Finding a parking space under a shady tree, Timothy cut off the engine and turned to his passenger. "So what's good, with you? What you wanna talk about?"

Shanae cocked her head to the side and squeezed her eyebrows together as she took him in. "The fuck you mean what I wanna talk about? You know damn well what's going on." She had no patience for him. His actions caused her to lose her man, her residence, and her overall peace of mind. "Look, let's cut the bull. I know you sent my man a letter talkin' shit about me but you said a whole lotta nothing. What the fuck you bringin' all that drama to my doorstep for?"

Timothy chuckled at the exasperated look on her face. He had to struggle not to burst out laughing at her act. Looking her straight in the eyes he stated, "Now you see, had I not been aware of your slutty ways I'd be falling for your innocent routine right now. But I know better Ms. Alexander. You acting like you gave a fuck about homeboy. What? You mad cuz somebody actually exposed you for the hoe you are?"

Shanae was stunned. Not because of the words he said, but because she never expected him to read her like that. She got on the defensive, "Who the fuck you calling a hoe? If I recall, you the married one stickin' your piece in anything that moves…"

"Which includes you, so you ain't no better," Timothy interrupted. A young couple sitting on a nearby bench glanced over at Timothy's Camry as the baritone in his voice carried through the open window.

"Look, let's keep it real. You and I fucked around; you took the bitch route and went running to my man, and shit. Then you gon' come over to me talking 'bout some 'we got some unfinished business.' What the fuck is that about? You played yourself." Shanae called herself setting things straight. "This shit is done, don't call me, don't text me, just leave me the fuck alone, okay!"

"Oooooh, so what you think you running things now?" Timothy folded his arms and leaned back against the driver side door, his signature smirk on full display. "I was tryin' to be nice but since you wanna be a bitch about it, here's the deal. You will fuck me when I want, how I want, with no complaints. You must have forgotten that I could've had your ass fired that day you pulled the stunt with the vacuums. What the fuck were you thinking anyway? You tryna do housekeeping on the side?" Timothy laughed aloud at his corny dig. "Not to mention all the niggas you be rappin' to all day at work. I had no idea you be fuckin' around like that

Shay, I gotta give you your props! Had me fooled thinking you were faithful to dude. So cut the shit, cuz this here is nothing. I'm actually doing you a favor since you love to fuck." He squeezed his crotch and took in her cleavage as tiny beads of sweat began to form at her bosom.

Shanae was annoyed, but not surprised that Timothy eavesdropped on her personal calls. She always hated the fact that the office cubicles provided no privacy. When the recent renovations were completed boasting shorter partitions, and the new seating arrangement called for Timothy to be her neighbor, Shanae didn't consider him being all up in her business. She actually thought there was something decent about him. How dumb of her! She studied his barber-fresh line up and blemish-free skin. He was a fine looking man, no doubt about that. There was no way she could risk unemployment with the situation she was in now. She needed to keep her job at AMP. Fuck it; I'ma find a way outta this shit with Tim. But in the meantime, I'll play his little game. I can't even front, he do have a big dick so at least I'll be getting something out of it! Her pussy jumped at the thought of riding him. She didn't trust herself enough to say anything, so she just cut her eyes and folded her arms over her chest. Timothy took that as a sign of defeat. He secured his seatbelt and started the engine. There was nothing left to say.

ENGLISH RULER

Chapter 3

The sound of horns blaring rang through the auditorium as Enur's 'Calabria' boomed through the high-powered speakers. "Easy now no need fi go down, easy now no need fi go down, rock dat run dat this where we're from."

Nicola and her dance class stomped across the stage and broke out into a fierce dance routine as proud friends and family looked on. Giselle, Lowell, Marcelle, Patrick, and his wife Suzie, watched from their seats in the packed balcony of Tarrytown High School.

"Watch mi girl," Patrick beamed as he watched Nicola perform a move where she dipped down to the floor, bent back, shimmied, and hopped back up in quick succession.

The dance routine was intricate and involved many specific and suggestive moves. Nicola's many evenings of practice paid off; the group put on an excellent performance. As the curtain closed the audience's standing ovation echoed off the theater walls. Giselle, Lowell, Marcelle, Patrick and Suzie slowly made their way through the crowded hallway, and downstairs to the gym where the dancers were changing into their street clothes.

"That was a really great show, Nicola has found her niche in dancing," Suzie smiled as she walked beside Giselle.

"I know. I'm so happy she found something she's interested in so early on. She's in her third year at Dance Pointe, and about to make her first year as part of the FLO Dance Team," Giselle gushed.

"Yah mon, mi likkle girl set fi big tings," Patrick was always a proud, supportive dad, even if he and Giselle couldn't make it work as man and wife.

"Me too, Dad, don't forget I'm gonna be the star athlete," Marcelle refused to be left out.

"Fi real?"

"Yup."

"And what sport are you gonna be playing?" Giselle inquired.

Marcelle cocked his head to the side as if in deep thought, "I'm not exactly sure just yet, but when I figure it out I'll be sure to get back to you."

"You is a likkle joker, nah true," Patrick stated and grabbed Marcelle around the neck playfully.

"Whaaat?" Marcelle asked innocently. They entered the gym and scanned the sea of people. Giselle spotted Nicola chatting with a few fellow dancers and their instructor, Ms. Kiara. When Nicola noticed her family, she abandoned the conversation and ran over to greet them. Patrick swallowed her in a huge embrace and told her how proud he was. Suzie and Marcelle handed her bouquets of roses as they also congratulated her on the show.

"Yes, she did an excellent job, one of my star pupils," Ms. Kiara said, smiling as she made her way over to the group. Although she had a host of pupils and families to deal with, she secretly admired Nicola's family and the support they provided her.

"Hi Ms. Kiara, how are you?" Giselle greeted her. "You know Lowell and Marcelle, and this is Patrick, Nicola's father, and his wife, Suzie." The group exchanged pleasantries.

"Ms. Frasier, I wanted to let you know personally that Nicola has been selected as one of the headlining performers for this summer's travel troupe."

Giselle opened her mouth in surprise and turned to Nicola, "You didn't tell me."

Nicola grinned shyly. "I wanted you and Dad to find out at the same time. And I knew he was coming so I asked Ms. Kiara to tell you guys…"

"This is fantastic, Nicola!" Giselle was ecstatic. She knew Nicola was counting on being chosen as part of the travel troupe, and she had spent the last few weeks encouraging her daughter not to put all her eggs in one basket. Nicola was driving everyone around her crazy with the possibility of not making it. Needless to say, this news was a breath of fresh air, not only for Nicola, but for the entire household as well.

"So celebration is definitely in order now, Cheesecake Factory anyone?" Lowell knew that was Nicola's favorite restaurant.

"You don't have to tell me twice," Nicola was elated.

"Well, I won't keep you all. Go out and have a good time. Nicola, make sure you give your mom the schedule I handed you earlier," Ms. Kiara said as she hugged Nicola. Then she turned to Giselle. "The tour starts at the end of June, but we're going to be performing at tri-state area schools to raise awareness in dance, and also to give the kids some practice. So I'll keep you posted on that as we haven't quite confirmed that schedule yet."

Giselle happily replied, "Thank you."

"It's that little hot stepper you have over there that deserves all the thanks and praise," Ms. Kiara noted. "It was nice to see you all again." They said their goodbyes before Ms. Kiara instructed Nicola to "Save me a piece of cheesecake."

The group exited the school hyped about Nicola's accomplishments. They stopped in the parking lot to sort out the driving arrangements to the restaurant. Nicola and Marcelle rode with Patrick and Suzie while Giselle and Lowell rode together in Lowell's Pathfinder.

After an enjoyable meal at the Cheesecake Factory, everyone drove back to Giselle and Lowell's so that Marcelle and Nicola could grab their clothes as they were staying with Patrick for the weekend. When the kids exited the car, Patrick followed. He walked with them up to the door.

"Hey, you 'ave a minute?" he asked Giselle who had just thrown her handbag down on the coffee table. Nicola and Marcelle raced upstairs to gather their overnight bags.

"Yeah come in, what's up?" Giselle asked as she perched her buttocks on the arm of the sofa. She was interested to know why Patrick was at her door when he could just as easily have waited in the car.

Patrick took in the living room décor as he got his words together. The walls were painted a soft pale green, and were accented with matching framed art pieces that complimented the new arrangement nicely. "Mi like di new set up, it look good."

"Thanks, it was time for a change." Giselle watched Patrick standing there awkwardly.

"Well mi just did waan tell you say Suzie pregnant, three months," Patrick said looking at Giselle for a reaction.

Giselle heard what he said, but it felt surreal. She knew when Patrick got married two years ago that there was a bigger chance her kids would be getting a sibling. She wasn't surprised Patrick hadn't had any more kids yet. One thing about him, he was not one to just lay his seed anywhere, and she'd always respected him for that. "Wow well I guess congratulations are in order," Giselle tried to let the smile she plastered on her face resonate in her voice. It wasn't that she was upset; she had no reason to be. She was simply taken off guard. "So when are you planning to tell the kids?" She inquired.

"This weekend, that's why mi did waan tell you first."

Just then, Marcelle rushed down the stairs, his overnight bag on one shoulder, and his XBox 360 console in its case in the opposite hand.

"You all packed and ready to go big man?" Giselle asked. "Yes ma'am, I've got my game I'm good."

"Yeah, I know you weren't about to forget it like last time," she reminded him.

"No way!"

"Okay, give me a hug, dad will be right out." Giselle kissed and hugged her son before he all but flew out the door. Turning her attention back to Patrick she said, "Well I'm sure they'll be happy. And Nicola is baby-sitting age so that's a plus right there." They both shared a laugh as Nicola made her way down the staircase with enough baggage to suffice a week's vacation.

"And what are you two laughing about?" She paused between her parents with one eyebrow raised questioningly.

Patrick grabbed her by the shoulder and steered her toward the door, "How much time me affi tell you? Likkle pickney nuh fi mix inna grown people business. You no hear?" Patrick playfully scolded his oldest child, then smiled and winked at Giselle.

"Daddy I'm fourteen, not exactly a 'likkle pickney' as you say..." Nicola was out the door with Patrick guiding the way.

"Bye Nic, I love you too," Giselle shouted out the door. Nicola tore away from her dad's clutch and ran back to bid her mom a proper farewell. "Love you Mom, see you Sunday."

"Love you too sweetie," Giselle said as she returned the hug Nicola offered.

"A'right then, so me an' you will chat if anything," Patrick said, following Nicola to the SUV.

"Ok, tell Suzie I'll call her," Giselle waited for them to pull away from the curb and waved them off. She closed and locked the door and began peeling away her clothes as she climbed the steps, anticipating a hot, soothing shower. She wondered what Lowell was occupied with that he hadn't come down to see the kids off, although she was sure they had exchanged goodbyes. Wait 'til he hears about Patrick and Suzie's pending arrival. She laughed to herself, and just as instantly – she became dead serious. Wonder if I'll be next. Lowell and I have to decide what we're doing. That should be me expecting…

Once Giselle crossed the threshold to her bedroom, she noticed Lowell sitting up on the bed staring into space. The TV was off; couple that with the kid-free household and you had an eerie silence.

"Hey, what's going on?" she asked.

Lowell looked at her and shook his head sadly. "Nothing, I guess," he replied then laid back, interlocked his fingers behind his head and focused on the ceiling.

When he did this, Giselle noticed the answering machine was stretched over from the night side table and pulled onto the bed. The message indicator was not blinking which meant that Lowell had already listened to any new messages that may have been left. Giselle threw her dirty garments into the hamper in the bathroom, put on her robe and went straight over to the machine. She decided against asking Lowell any more questions and hit play.

"You have four saved messages…" The automated voice filled the silence in the room. "First saved message: Hey Lowell, its Marc, give me a call when you have a minute." Beep. Second saved message: "Good afternoon this message is for Lowell Washington. Mr. Washington this is Evelyn from Dr.

Garcia's office. Please give us a call; it's regarding your test results from last week's appointment." Beep. "Third saved message…"

Giselle stopped the machine. She was sure the cause of Lowell's foul mood was due to the last message from Dr. Garcia's office. Lowell had finally had enough of her constant badgering about going to the doctors. He allowed her to schedule an appointment, the previous Thursday, and she had accompanied him to see his primary care physician. She didn't enter the examination room but she knew that his doctor had performed several blood and urine tests. He even had to go back on Monday to take an additional blood test for which he had to fast for eight hours prior. Although medical professionals are not allowed to leave any sort of defining news on an answering machine, the call just didn't feel like good news to Giselle. As she looked over at the worry on Lowell's face, it was obvious he felt he same way. She sat beside him on their queen size bed and took his hand in hers.

"Honey, what are you thinking right now, that it's bad news? You won't know anything until you call them back," she said gently.

"I know, but Dr. Garcia's not back in 'til Monday."

Giselle fought back the smile that threatened to claim her lips due to Lowell's child-like tone.

"Right, so are you gonna fret every second up until then? We actually have this weekend kid-free and you want to consume yourself with the possibility of bad news. I have no problem keeping your mind occupied you know. So we can just enjoy ourselves this weekend and deal with whatever Monday brings us on Monday," she said giving him a small smile.

The soft glow of the lamp brought out the golden highlights of her medium-length flat-ironed hair. Lowell ran his eyes over every feature of her pretty face. Her light brown complexion, full cheeks, freshly waxed eyebrows, and gloss-tinted lips all came together as a beautiful piece of artwork to him. However, at that moment he didn't focus on her beauty because the love she had for him was emanating from her being. He pulled her down next to him and laid her head on his chest. Damn I love this woman!

Finding the opening to her robe, he slipped his hand beneath the fabric and caressed her naked belly. "Keeping me occupied takes a lot of work. Are you sure you're up for the challenge?" He asked, shifting his hand to tend to her left breast.

"I'm always up for a good challenge, and why does it sound like you doubt my skills?" asked Giselle with mild sass. Her eyes were now closed and she was enjoying Lowell's slow, deliberate touch.

"Talking about skills, I have a few of my own ya know," Lowell claimed before repositioning himself to face her. Their lips met, and the warmth of his tongue entered her mouth. Giselle leaned into the kiss and enclosed him in her arms. He felt comfort in her embrace and wished to be no other place in the world.

Notwithstanding the physical pleasure he was experiencing, mental anguish remained. There was no getting around the fact that he had a serious health problem. The doctor ran tests to rule out conditions such as high blood pressure, diabetes, and liver disease. In addition, the secret he had been withholding would soon have to be revealed, changing his life indefinitely. He never viewed at Giselle as a "ride or die" chick. But he hoped now more than ever that she was one!

Chapter 4

"So what are you saying, what time are you gonna reach here?" Maxine inquired as she balanced the phone between her shoulder and right ear. She was on the edge of her bed painting her toenails with a shiny burgundy polish.

"I don't know. Whenever I'm finished with Rhianne, she's been asking me to come over all week. I'll probably end up taking her shopping at Bay Plaza, and then maybe to the movies, we'll see," Shanae replied as she slipped her size eight feet into a pair of jeweled thongs.

She was preparing to visit her sister's house and spend some quality time with her only niece. Being an auntie was special to Shanae and she hated to disappoint Rhianne. With all that had been going on with Tremaine and having to move, she had not been over Melanie's in almost three weeks. A visit to her sister's was long overdue.

"Whatever…just make sure you bring your butt over here; I want some company. Quincy is about to go over his boy's house, so we'll have the place to ourselves."

Shanae kissed her teeth. "Yeah, okay. At least you have male company. Shoot, if I had that I'd be straight." She missed the comfort and security of having Tremaine in her life. He had not answered any of her calls, nor had he called her. Of course, this was to be expected. Shanae knew there was a zero chance of rekindling their relationship, but for her own piece of mind, she wanted to at least part on decent terms. Truth be told, there was no guilt, she just didn't want Tremaine to stay angry with her. Once again another testament to her consistent selfishness.

Maxine rolled her eyes, "Well in that case, bring your crooked ass over here ASAP. Call when you're close. Later."

Shanae disconnected the call and grabbed her knock off Louis Vuitton messenger bag before shutting off the TV and grabbing her keys. As she locked her room door, her housemate, Yesenia, was coming up the steps with her 11-month-old son, Rudi. Shanae went over and assisted with the stroller; the baby was fast asleep, and Yesenia was struggling with groceries as well.

"Thanks Shanae. This boy is getting so heavy. I'll be happy when he starts walking on his own." Yesenia was a nineteen year old single mother who took up residence in the boarding house when her mother kicked her out due to her pregnancy. She'd been living there going on a year now, but worked a full-time job and took online classes to improve her situation. Shanae respected the fact that she was trying to better herself.

"You're welcome, Yessy. Oh by the way, the toilet is actin' up. Mrs. Jofield claims she's sending someone up to look at it today. I haven't seen Jay, so if you happen to see him mention it please."

Jay was the third and final tenant to round out the second floor of the boarding house. He was a middle-aged, openly gay, bi-racial man (Black and Puerto Rican) who rarely held his tongue. His animated, flamboyant ways and witty humor always brought smiles to the Shanae and Yesenia's faces. The three of them got along well, which was a good thing since they had to share such limited space.

"No prob," Yesenia stated as she worked her key into the lock of her room door. "I think he's away for a few days doing one of his drag shows, though."

"Oh ok, well I'll see you later," Shanae called over her shoulder as she bounced down the stairs.

£

The Colonial style home located at 157 Court Street in White Plains, New York boasted a handsome Maple tree, manicured hedges, and a stunning sod lawn. Shanae's 2007 Toyota Camry pulled into the stamped concrete driveway behind a fully loaded Infinity G37 Sedan.

Before she could make her way out of the vehicle, a caramel complexioned young girl with long intricately styled cornrows shot out the front door. She was sharply dressed in a printed navy and white short set with low cut sneakers and socks. Her matching wristlet let it be known that this was a young diva in the making.

"Hi Aunt Shay, I'm ready," she exclaimed, all smiles as she reached the driver's side door.

Shanae laughed as she viewed her niece through the glass window. Exiting the car, she enclosed Rhianne in a tight hug. "You're a hot mess girl. You know I have to see your mom first." They strolled up the walkway and into the house.

The aroma of savory garlic filtered through Shanae's nostrils as she crossed the threshold of Melanie's home. Melanie was a self-proclaimed "foodie" and prided herself on whipping up delicious meals. It was a regular thing to see her slicing and dicing as she often experimented in her kitchen.

"Hey Sis," Shanae gave her big sister a hug and a peck on the cheek.

"Hey you, what's going on?"

"Nothing much, still tryin' to get used to the new place, you know…"

"How is it over there anyway? You know you could have stayed here, I don't know why you're acting up." Naturally, Melanie always felt the need to protect her little sister.

41

"You know I wasn't tryna impose on you and Randy like that. Plus, staying in that God-awful house will force me to get my shit together." Shanae took a seat at the breakfast nook.

Melanie noticed Rhianne hanging onto Shanae's every word and felt she needed to be excused. She had no patience for children who inserted themselves into adult conversation.

"Rhianne, why don't you go and continue folding the laundry on your bed until your Aunt Shay is ready."

"Okay," Rhianne reluctantly retreated upstairs to her room.

With child ears out of the way, Melanie asks, "So what's the real deal, how are you holding up with all this sudden change?"

"I'm all right. You know, there's nothing I can do but move on," Shanae shrugged her shoulders.

"I agree, but how do you plan to do that? It's me your talking to you know, I know how you do!" Melanie stated, looking pointedly at her sister.

Shanae rolled her eyes, "Anyway, I'm not even tryna stay in that house. Sharing the bathroom and kitchen is not cute. I'm hoping to be out of there in a few months tops. A decent studio or one-bedroom apartment would do me just fine."

"Okay, so how's your financial situation, do you need anything?"

Melanie was aware that Shanae did not make a lot of money. As a licensed physical therapist specializing in sports medicine, Melanie did well for herself and was willing to help Shanae out when needed. At the same time, she always encouraged her to get out there and take the proper steps to secure her future. She often marveled at the fact that although they grew up in the same home under the same supervision, they were so very different. Melanie was a goal setter and extremely organized; everything she had ever done was planned out, whereas Shanae thought about issues as they arose. She didn't even know how to save and never took the time to invest in anything long enough to see what hard work and patience could produce.

"Nah, I'm good. I'll make do."

"What does that mean? I'm not gonna beg to give you a loan, I'm saying if you need something you need to say so."

"No really, I'm all right. Thanks though." Shanae could have used a few bucks, but she didn't feel like taking anything from Melanie. She had done so much for Shanae already. It seemed like every time she turned around Melanie was bailing her out of something.

"I hear you, but if you're really hurtin'…"

"Thanks, Mel."

"Of course!"

"What's going on with you? Where's Ray?"

"He's working overtime. You know he's a workaholic," Melanie said as she sliced mushrooms with chef-like precision.

"I gotta give you your props, I don't know how you cop wives do it. I'd be a wreck every time my man went to work."

"You just have to look at it as a job or you'll drive yourself crazy. When we were dating, I'd be nervous as hell while he was working, but by the time we married, I was used to it. Plus he's got six years of service under his belt and has never had a serious incident, thank God."

"Thank God is right!" Shanae replied as she checked a notification on her cell phone. "Fuckin' asshole," she muttered under her breath when she recognized the sender as Timothy.

"What's wrong?"

"Ah, nothing. Stupid forwards," Shanae lied as she pocketed her phone.

She hadn't confided in anyone about her situation with Timothy. He was becoming quite aggressive with his demands, making it a point to have most of their quickies in secluded areas of the office during business hours. The thrill of being caught and the fear Shanae displayed only heightened his excitement. Shanae was almost positive that Maxine knew what was going on.

More than once, she caught Maxine giving her odd looks in the office. Timothy always made Shanae 'wander off' first and then he'd follow her, no doubt making their 'private' meetings blatantly obvious. Maxine and Shanae were cool, but Shanae hadn't decided if she'd confide in her; she wanted to see if she could handle it on her own for now. If she told her about that problem, she may have to come clean about other things that Maxine may not be so receptive of. In her mind, it's best to cross that bridge when she gets to it.

"Well, let me get out of here, we're gonna hit up Bay Plaza, see how much damage we can do," Shanae stood and stretched her tight limbs.

"Bay Plaza? There is nothing up there for Rhianne. You're better off going to the Galleria; at least they have her stores there. You know she can stay all day in Claire's and Justice alone."

"Yeah, that's true. Plus, it's closer."

Shanae walked over to the bottom of the steps and called for Rhianne to come down. Rhianne hurried down the stairs, her braids jiggling about her shoulders along the way.

"A'ight Sis, we'll be back in a couple of hours."

"Okay."

"Bye Mom," Rhianne yelled from the doorway, eager for quality time with her only aunt.

"See you later, RiRi," Melanie called as she made her way over to lock the door.

Chapter 5

The Galleria Mall was the place to shop in White Plains. Of course, there was The Westchester, but that was considered strictly high end featuring stores like Neiman Marcus, Gucci, Salvatore Ferragamo, and Louis Vuitton.

Shanae and Rhianne made their way to every corner of The Galleria, tried on several outfits, and sprayed random fragrances before settling at a wobbly table in the food court. Over lunch, Shanae was pleased to hear that Rhianne was still on the honor roll and now interested in participating in school funded extra-curricular activities.

"So what did you have in mind? Sports or choir or something like that?" Shanae asked between bites of her gyro.

Rhianne was enjoying her chicken nuggets and fries courtesy of Wendy's. "Not sports, maybe drama or dance. We had an assembly the other day saying that the schools are trying to get the kids interested in other things besides sports. They sent a letter home and Mom said I need to pick something since I've never participated."

At ten years old, Rhianne was very bright and well-spoken. She brought home good grades regularly, and rarely gave Melanie and Ray a hard time. Shanae found Melanie to be an attentive and caring mother; she could only hope to be that good of a mother when her time came.

"Well that sounds good. You'll have to let me know so I could come and watch your events."

"Okay."

Once they completed their meals, the pair indulged in fifteen minute massages in high powered vending chairs the mall provided before putting an end to their shopping experience.

After Rhianne was dropped off at home with her new purchases, Shanae headed over to Maxine's for some adult company. Maxine lived in the Wakefield section of the Bronx, not too far from the Mt. Vernon apartment that Shanae had shared with Tremaine. It was a busy area with all modes of transportation readily available, including boot-leg cabs. Though the area was mainly inhabited by Blacks and Hispanics, there were a handful of Whites sprinkled throughout. Maxine had been living in the fast-paced neighborhood for over three years and was right at home with her multi-cultural loving self.

Shanae parked her car and as she approached Maxine's building, she could hear Nikki Minaj's 'Super Bass' pumping through an open window. She looked up and to no surprise the music was coming from Maxine's kitchen window. Shanae crossed the threshold of the lobby, bypassing the broken front door, and making her way up two flights of stairs to Maxine's apartment.

"About time, beeyotch!" was Maxine's greeting when she flung open the door.

"Look at you, looks like you already started getting nice," Shanae commented as she took a seat on the living room sofa. Maxine was dressed in a pair of cut-off jean shorts and a tank top. Her brunette-reddish hair sat in a loose bun on top of her head; a smoldering blunt between her red lips.

"Can't be waitin' on your slow ass or I'd be walkin' around sober and shit. You already know!" Maxine stayed twisted. Her vices were weed and moscato or vice versa, any order would be correct. She was a fun-loving twenty-three year old who enjoyed the single life. She and Shanae hit it off at work instantly, but when they started hanging out outside of the office and realized they shared a love of men and weed, well, they were inseparable after that. The only difference was that while Shanae cheated and dealt with married men, Maxine was into one man at a time.

"Yeah, yeah so where my glass at?"

"Please! You ain't no stranger, find your way to the kitchen and stop playin.'" Maxine curled her legs under her as she got comfortable in her leather recliner.

Shanae followed Maxine's orders and retrieved a wine glass from the kitchen cabinet. She poured herself a drink and joined Maxine in the living room. A fat bag of 'kush'weed was sitting on the coffee table with a pack of Backwoods.

Maxine tossed both to Shanae and instructed her, "Twist somethin' up."

"Dang, you full of demands today, huh," Shanae joked. She knew once Maxine was into her own blunt, she would have to build her own or pry the other one from Maxine's cold, dead fingers.

Maxine used the remote to switch the song on the ipod Dock from Sean Paul's "Temperature" to Teena Marie's 'Square Biz.' She pranced around her living room dancing to the 80's hit and singing along with Motown's own "Vanilla Child."

"I got the best, the most, baby from coast to coast, and I don't wanna boast but I love you square biz, I'm talkin' square biz to ya baby, square, square biz, I'm talkin love that is, square, square biz."

Maxine loved all types of music but she was most at home listening to R & B. Growing up, almost all her mother's friends were Black, and she has always lived in neighborhoods that had a predominantly Black population, so it was natural for her to become accustomed to the African American culture. Her love life was no exception; Maxine could count on one hand how many Caucasian men she'd dated. And that was just fine because Black men loved her; not only did she have ass and shape for a white girl, she was down-to-earth, easy to get along with, and she knew how to handle herself in any situation. Maxine was book smart, but it was her street smarts that gained the respect of her Black peers. Some mistook her up-front mannerisms as ghetto, but really, with Maxine what you saw was what you got. She had no time to pull punches; this was one of the reasons she got along so well with Shanae.

Shanae lit a fire under the freshly rolled blunt and inhaled the smoke deep into her lungs. She held it in for a brief moment and then released it in two streams of smoke through her nostrils. Grabbing her glass, she sat back in the sofa and watched Maxine channel Teena Marie, an empty Corona bottle acting as her mic.

Circling the sofa, Maxine grooved to the funky tune, pulling a relaxed Shanae to her feet to be a part of the impromptu performance. Contrary to popular belief, Maxine may be white, but she could dance her ass off. She was able to keep up with the best of them. The two friends broke it down to a few more hits before collapsing on the sofa, spent.

"Oh my gosh that was so much fun," Maxine said catching her breath.

"Yes it was, I can't even front, you be buggin' out," Shanae laughed.

"Music is the key to my soul; I swear I came out of my mother's womb dancing!"

They shared a laugh.

"So how was Bay Plaza?"

"We ended up going to the Galleria. I think we went in every store twice, that child is too much," Shanae said, recalling how Rhianne behaved like a little woman accepting the various samples during their excursion.

"You went to the Galleria? Hold up, I know you picked me up something from that little gadget store I love," Maxine was poised to attack Shanae with a throw pillow.

"Girl, how many Snuggies and Shamwows do you need?"

"Whatever, I don't hear you complainin' when you wanna borrow my shit though," Maxine was a faithful customer of 'As Seen on TV', the mall version of a mail order store.

Shanae chuckled as the pillow connected with her head. Maxine found this to be a good opportunity to address something she noticed a while ago.

"You know what, on a serious note, wassup with you and Timothy? I've been seeing you and him actin' kinda suspect around the office lately," Maxine asked pointedly, taking a drag off her blunt.

Shanae pondered the inquiry, however briefly, but it was still evident that she was contemplating being entirely forthcoming.

"Taking too long too answer is the first indication that you're preparing to tell a lie. Remember you can keep it one hundred with me. There are no judgments from ya girl."

Shanae was tired of carrying around the burden of bad decisions and snowballed lies. She looked Maxine in the face and blurted out, "I fucked up...really fucked up."

Maxine waited expectantly for Shanae's dramatics to begin. They had been bff's for over two years and she was used to Shanae embellishing situations for the sake of sympathy. "What's up?"

"Well you know Tremaine and I ain't together no more, but what I never told you was that it was because I cheated with Tim," Shanae stated.

Maxine's face bore a "what the fuck" expression.

"Before you even say anything, let me finish. I know this guy that started a cleaning business, something like Merry Maids, and I told him that I had the hookup with some vacuums. I was only planning to take two, but he needed more and I figured I could make some quick change, so I started taking more. Long story short, Tim saw me on the loading dock with two Dysons and pretty much caught me red handed," Shanae explained.

"Okay, so what does…"

"Hold up, let me finish. That nicca was talking about reporting me and getting me fired, so I started fuckin' him and have been ever since. Thing is, I never knew Mr. Hoffman got the cameras replaced as part of the renovation; they put new fuckin' cameras in the old housing! So the time I got away with the vacuums is all caught on tape. All Tim needs to do is have HR run it," Shanae concluded.

Maxine couldn't believe her ears. "Are you fuckin' kidding me? He's blackmailing you?" She went to take a hard drag off her blunt, which was now out due to her lack of pulls while she was engrossed in Shanae's story; she opted for a swig of moscato instead. "And AMP is slick too; they paid how much thousands on renovations but wanna save a few bucks on camera housing, what the fuck! How do you know he's telling the truth about the cameras though?"

"You know Chrissy is careless with taking things off the community printer. I saw the bill on there the other day."

Maxine shook her head. "I don't know why they have her careless ass paying the bills. Janice would be pissed if she found out she was leaving financials on the printer. I keep telling her we need our own;

accounting should not be sharing with customer service. But back to that asshole…blackmail?"

"Yeah that motherfucka is blackmailing me. But that's not the worst part…I got pregnant fuckin' with that nicca and had an abortion. He found out and wrote a letter to Tremaine talkin' about how I'm a hoe and a whole bunch of other shit."

"Shut up!" Maxine bellowed.

"No joke. Dude was eavesdropping on all my calls at work and everything; knew all the business. Tremaine showed up to take me to my follow-up appointment, compliments of Tim. That was pretty much how it all ended with me and him – in the clinic examination room."

"I can't believe what I'm hearing right now." Maxine was in shock. Although she didn't know Tremaine well, she was cordial with him during phone calls to the house. She and Quincy had even hung out with him and Shanae once and she found him to be a nice guy. Maybe a little too nice for Shanae she thought at times. It had come up once during conversation, that he couldn't have children, and this fact crossed Maxine's mind as she thought the situation over. "And I'm sure the whole clinic situation was just too much for Tremaine…" she said.

"Girl, I almost died. He took it hard, of course. But there's nothing I can do to change the reality of the situation. I mean, I'm not proud of what I did to him, but it is what it is, and it just turned out to be a fucked up sequence of events." Shanae was just a little too passive with the situation for Maxine's taste.

"You really sound like a cold-hearted bitch," Maxine said, her voice rising with disbelief.

"Come on Maxine what was I supposed to do?" Shanae asked starting to pace aimlessly around the room.

"You were supposed to not take the freakin' vacuums. You were supposed to not fuck him. Come on Shay, you may not want to hear this but, you know I'm gonna tell you like it is." Maxine was serious, and Shanae really didn't give a shit.

"I've just gotta figure out how to get out of this mess," Shanae plopped herself onto the sofa, threw her head back and closed her eyes. In her mind, it wasn't the fact that she was in a bind, it was just how she got out of it that mattered.

Maxine loved her friend, but she was tired of her making careless decisions. Just as Maxine was about to tell her as much, her landline rang.

"Hello…"

Shanae studied the fibers of the carpeting as Maxine engaged the caller.

"Nothing, just here with Shay bullshittin'," Maxine stated as she glanced at her friend. "Of course I'm goin' to work tomorrow…listen to you sounding like someone's father."

Shanae shook her head; it was obviously Quincy calling to be nosey. Maxine got up to take their empty glasses to the kitchen sink. "Well what time is that?" She inquired of the caller as she re-entered the living room. "Don't even think of walking in here at some ungodly hour, and don't worry about us we're grown." Maxine glanced at the cable box for the time. This wasn't lost on Shanae. "Goodbye, Quincy." Slight attitude dripped from her tone as she disconnected the line. She looked at Shanae. "He gets on my damn nerves."

"But you love it."

"I can say that I do, I can say that I do. But back to you, you've gotta remedy that situation and quick. Tim is not one to be leaving in control of things. I don't trust his ass and right now he's running the show."

"I know. I'm gonna find a way to work this out," Shanae offered as she stepped into the bathroom. When she re-entered the living room she noticed it was after nine.

"I'm gonna head out. Start preparing for the plantation tomorrow."

"Tell me about it. Quincy says he won't be in 'til late, so I'm gonna shower and call it a night myself as well."

Shanae gathered her keys and bag, "I'll see you tomorrow Max, we can do lunch."

"Okay girl, see you in the morning," Maxine said as she let Shanae out and secured the door behind her.

£

The exotic scent of Avon's Haiku lingered in the air as Shanae laid out her work clothes for the following day. She was tired from the day's outings, but was refreshed after taking a long, hot shower.

Grabbing her gray pumps, she placed them with the gray pantsuit and lavender blouse on the recliner for easy access in the morning. She crossed the room to her bed and settled in under the covers.

Flipping through the channels, she stopped on Tamar Braxton of Braxton Family Values having one of her 'dotcom' rants. As Tamar and her sister Traci argued on the screen, Shanae thought she heard her doorbell. She muted the TV and listened, silence. She pressed the mute button again and tried to get back into the show when her cell phone rang. Who the hell...

Shanae's heart skipped a beat when she saw the caller's number. "Hello?"

"Wassup Shanae, I'm downstairs come open the door," the caller said calmly.

"What are you doing here?"

"Come open the door and stop playing."

Shanae signed audibly and disconnected the call. She quickly got up and took stock of herself in the dresser mirror. She had on a baby tee and terrycloth lounge pants which she quickly covered with her robe.

When she reached the front door, she looked through the peephole and saw her guest waiting for her with his hands in his pant pockets. Although she didn't want to let him in, she didn't want to take the chance of someone seeing him on her doorstep at such an odd hour either. She released the locks, swung open the door, and stepped aside.

"Wassup," the man said as he stepped inside and walked straight up to her room as if he owned the place. Shanae locked the door and followed him, closing her bedroom door behind her. She stood there and watched her guest sitting comfortably on her bed.

He smiled, "What's wrong? Come here," he motioned for her to come with his head.

"You know you shouldn't be here," Shanae said, holding onto her spot in the middle of the room. He walked over to her, grabbed her by the back of her head and stuck his tongue in her mouth. His thick, soft tongue stirred Shanae's libido and she involuntarily gave in to the kiss. Large, strong hands roamed her body and found their way beneath her robe as she enjoyed the taste of his mouth. Garments were being shed at breakneck speed and before

Shanae knew it, she was flipped onto the bed in nothing but her stud earrings.

She looked up into his lustful eyes, all she could think was, what kind of friend am I? Quincy was oblivious to her thoughts and proceeded with his goal of getting a blow job and some ass. He stood before Shanae, member erect, and guided her head to his manhood. Without hesitation, Shanae explored her fellatio skills, sucking, licking, and slurping as she thought back to how she wound up creeping with her friend's man.

It wasn't intentional, although Shanae had the opportunity to rectify the situation – she didn't. This twist of fate happened about four months ago when a clean shaven, fair-skinned UPS driver approached the entrance to the AMP office building as Shanae made her exit to grab lunch.

They crossed paths in the walkway.

He asked, "Excuse me, can I talk to you for a minute?"

All Shanae saw was a good looking man in uniform with no ring on his finger, but who was she kidding? She would have went for hers ring or not! Had she been more level-headed, she would have noticed that he did not have a package in his possession to deliver.

It only took a few phone calls and on their first real meeting, they took it to the next level and have been messing around ever since. Shanae had no idea she was doing anything wrong; Maxine had told her about some guy she was seeing, but never went into detail.

When Shanae and Quincy first fucked, he told her that he was "talking" to someone – nothing serious. Shanae being the woman she is didn't care anyway, but imagine her chagrin when she stopped by Maxine's one day and witnessed Quincy stepping out of Maxine's bedroom. To her credit, Shanae played it off well and kept her shock in check during the introductions. On the other hand, Quincy's smug expression was lost on Maxine who was excited at finally introducing her friend to her new boo.

Needless to say, Shanae missed the opportunity to be forthcoming and let her friend know what kind of lowlife scum bucket she was dealing with. Furthermore, in missing that chance, Shanae also set the stage for more lies, secrecy, and for Quincy to have his cake and eat it, too.

Chapter 6

Lowell always prided himself on being strong, athletic, and able-bodied. He wasn't familiar with the current feelings of weakness and fatigue but it was something that he would need to deal with given his poor health.

A former Major in the US Army, he'd always been big on fitness and endurance. His drive both physically and mentally has always pushed him; he went from being a part-time Army Reservist to serving full-time due to the war. He enjoyed the military regimen, so once he completed his online college courses and earned his degree in Engineering, he went from being a Sergeant to Officer Candidate School and became a Lieutenant. He rose in rank over the next few years, eventually leading his battalion in his final rank as Major. He enjoyed his current career as an Aviation Engineer for National Airlines and could not envision himself unable to perform his required duties.

Laying on the chaise lounge in the living room, Lowell pondered Dr. Garcia's diagnosis. Type 2 Diabetes. The news devastated Lowell and crushed his spirit. He of all people should have been aware of the signs; his mother died of the illness when he was twenty-two years old. To say this scared Lowell

62

would be an understatement, he was terrified. Dr. Garcia was unable to determine a prognosis and insisted that further tests for be taken. To treat his illness Lowell was ordered to monitor his blood sugar, exercise regularly, and maintain a healthy diet.

Giselle rid the fridge of fatty foods, then went out and bought fresh fruits and vegetables, fish, chicken breasts, whole wheat products, and other healthy foods to support Lowell's change in diet. The mood of the house was sullen; everyone felt uneasy due to the unpredictability of Lowell's condition.

Nicola was excited about her upcoming travel showcases. She spent much of her free time practicing the routines and preparing to represent her troop. Lowell was one of her biggest supporters and she hoped he would be able to make all of her shows. It was weird for her to be so amped about something and not have Lowell and Giselle as her in-house cheering squad. Even Marcelle was flying under the radar these days. Lowell knew everyone was concerned for him, but he also didn't want them stressing either. It had been a week since his diagnosis and he and Giselle noticed the shift in the vibe of the house and agreed to make a concerted effort to keep things upbeat.

Although Lowell was having issues, they did not want that to be something the kids worried about and took on as their own. They agreed to keep

Marcelle and Nicola abreast of things without alarming them. The truth was at that point as long as Lowell kept his diet and exercise regimen under control, and monitored his blood sugar, he should be fine. He was aware of what he had to do; he just had to put it into action.

Lowell got up off the chaise and went to see what the kids were doing; Giselle was at the gym as was her usual routine three out of five days after work. Lowell passed Marcelle's bedroom to find him playing Call of Duty: Modern Warfare on Xbox Live. He continued on to Nicola's room where she was messing around on Facebook. He decided to engage her and find out why everyone and their mother were on the Facebook frenzy.

"Facebook! Tell me, what's so great about this thing that has everyone signing up for an account?"

Nicola laughed as she looked at Lowell leaning against her bedroom doorframe, arms crossed over his broad chest.

"Well, it's only the greatest thing since sliced bread, and a great way to stay in touch with your friends and family that you don't get to see all the time. You can even find people you want to reconnect with. I been told you let me set up an account for you."

"I'm not letting you sucker me into the whole social networking thing, no thank you."

"See look at you sounding old. You sound like Mom! Ya'll are gonna have to get with the times ya know."

"You did not call me the "O" word little girl. I'll show you old, sign me up for one of those MyFace accounts!" Lowell purposely said the name wrong. He pulled up a chair next to Nicola's computer.

"For real? Cool, let's do it."

For the next hour, Nicola helped Lowell set up a Facebook account complete with profile picture and she as his first friend. When it came time for Lowell to find friends he simply started with co-workers and a few friends he already knew had accounts.

"You only have nine friends, Low. You know more people than that. Facebook is for finding people; what about your old military boys or old schoolmates?"

Lowell thought for a second and found a few old military associates. He thought of a few names from high school, and once Facebook started suggesting friends based on the ones he had already added, and Nicola showed him how easy it was to find friends of friends, it was a wrap!   Before it was all over, Lowell had twenty-one friends added and thirty-five more friend requests pending approval. He quickly got caught up in looking at people's photos and how much they had changed over the years.

Nicola watched him scroll through the albums and different profiles. "See how easy it is to get caught up? Mmm mmm mmph, I hate to yell you, you're a Facebook junkie already," she declared, shaking her head.

"How you figure that?"

"Look at you already navigating it like a pro. But for real though, I find people I went to kindergarten with and it's crazy and I'm still in school, so I know for you it must be wild!"

Lowell had to turn and look at her in the face after that statement. "Where did you see that I made kindergarten connections?" He laughed out while shaking his head at her youthful flippancy.

"You know what I mean," she started.

"Yes I do. This thing is pretty genius, I'm not gonna lie. Hey, write down my password and stuff so I don't forget it, at least until I get used to it," Lowell said as he got up from around the PC. Nicola jotted down his login information and handed it to him.

"Thanks, Nic. I hope I didn't just let you sucker me a new obsession."

"Only time will tell," Nicola's voice trailed him teasingly as he exited her room. Walking toward the room he shared with Giselle, Lowell fingered the slip of paper in his pocket. At first he didn't think anything of the Facebook thing but when Nicola said it was for finding people he thought that maybe this was the tool he needed to start the process of reconciling his past.

£

Penny Starks never considered herself to be an ugly woman, average maybe, but certainly not ugly. Her brown paper bag complexion was riddled with blemishes that had darkened over the years and her teeth weren't as white as they were in her wedding photos, but she knew her straight hair and grey eyes had to count for something. It was the one thing she could guarantee that everyone would complement her on throughout her life, because they always did. And it was exactly what Timothy had complimented her on when she stopped long enough for him to ask her for her number as she rang up his purchase in Wal-Mart all those years ago.

This is why she couldn't understand why her husband was sending sex-filled text messages to his trampy co-worker. She clutched his cell phone in her sweaty hands while her moist fingertips scrolled through the various messages. The outgoing texts were consistently raunchy, while the responses were simple and to the point, never inviting or reciprocal. What ate at Penny's soul was the fact that there were several pictures of "Sexy Shay" stored on her husband's personal device. Her jealous haze didn't allow her to rationalize that none of the photos were posed for, nor did the subject seem to have knowledge of the camera's presence. All she saw was that her muffin top and cellulite-riddled thighs couldn't compete with the curvaceous shape that seemed to fill out every outfit the camera captured Shanae in.

Timothy bathed under the hot, steady spray of water his bathroom's showerhead offered, clueless to the violation of his privacy taking place only feet away. Penny wasn't too bright, but where there's a will, common sense kicks in.

From watching Timothy handle his phone, she knew that when he closed it she would have at least two minutes to access it before the security feature kicked in. Lucky for her, he received a call on his way into the shower. He answered it and spoke briefly with his brother Larry then went right in the bathroom leaving his phone on the bedside table.

Penny was like a tiger pouncing on its prey as soon as she heard the water start. She knew Timothy would go ballistic if he caught her with his phone, but she also knew she needed answers. Her husband cheated, that was nothing new. The difference this time was that it seemed as though there was only one woman. Penny took that to mean it was something serious and decided to intervene to stake claim on what was hers. She was somewhat familiar with the staff of AMP as she had attended the annual holiday parties over the years. She never had a reason to pay attention to any of the females there before now; the only memory that came to mind was last December's holiday party where she recalled Shanae on the dance floor at one point with a nice looking guy. I don't know if that bitch has a man or not. All I know is she better keep her hands off mine. An office love affair was not something Penny was about to tolerate, at all.

£

The scent of sex was thick in the air. Muffled groans, grunts and light slapping sounds were indication to any passerby that some sexual tensions were being relieved within the dark stock room. Shanae's foot was propped on a shelf of cleaning products while she used her hands to steady herself against the cool wall as Timothy pounded away at her from behind.

"Mmm, damn Shanae, throw it back. Put this big ass to good use." Perspiration lined his forehead as he gripped her waist firmly, making sure to sink his member as deep into her as possible.

Shanae rolled her eyes in the dark room. Just shut the fuck up and finish, she thought. She had twenty minutes to go before her shift started and she needed to slip out of the housekeeping closet unnoticed in order to freshen up before clocking in. These were the awkward situations she found herself in messing with Timothy. They'd arrived to work half an hour early to make use of the supply closet. Timothy had a thing for public sex and Shanae had no choice in the matter as his unwilling participant.

Wrapping up their most recent session, Timothy eyed Shanae as she adjusted her skirt, "That was good Shay, just what I needed this morning."

Shanae couldn't stand his ass. If she didn't like him before, she certainly despised him now. The twisted affair between the two of them had been going on for several weeks and Shanae wasn't sure how much more she could take. She had even started browsing job listings in hopes of leaving the company to escape Timothy. In her mind, there was no other way out of the predicament. Once she was sure she looked presentable, Shanae slowly peeked out the closet. Located in the alcove between the main office and warehouse, it was not in a high traffic area, so the coast was clear. The couple made their exit heading in opposite directions.

Refreshed and sitting at her desk, Shanae threw herself into her work but with Timothy sitting only feet away, it was difficult for her to concentrate. It didn't make sense to request a new seating arrangement because that would raise questions. Besides, new seating wouldn't alleviate the blackmailing. Temporary relief came at twelve o'clock by way of lunch. Shanae, Maxine, and Trudy, another AMP employee, took a short walk down the street to Molly's Café. While they ate, they made small talk and exchanged company gossip.

"Oh my goodness, did ya'll see Robyn come back from lunch last Wednesday? She was toasted out of her mind! That girl really needs to stop having liquid lunches, it's sad," Shanae commented.

"I saw that…" Maxine took a bite of her roasted turkey Panini and shook her head.

Trudy added her piece, "I guess you all didn't see her in Jobeth's office two days ago."

Shanae and Maxine gave her their attention.

"Nooooo…" they replied in unison.

Trudy relished the attention. She pushed herself away from the table slightly and crossed her thick legs, "Well, let's just say that it was immediately after lunch, Jobeth didn't even give her time to go in the bathroom so you know her breath was stank." Shanae and Maxine cracked up at that comment. Trudy had to join in too, although she meant every word. "Y'all know what I mean, anyway so Jobeth had her in there for close to half an hour. When she came out her eyes were all red, so it had to be serious."

Maxine was shaking her head, "Serious would have been Jobeth taking her drunk ass in to HR. I'd like to see the day she stops taking up for her employees and covering shit up."

Shanae shrugged her shoulders and sipped her lemonade, "I'm not even worried about that lush, 'cause trust me, one day a salesman is gonna be visiting the office and put her on full blast, and Jobeth's not gonna be able to do anything about it at that point. Mark my words." The ladies chitchatted for a while longer before walking back to the office.

As they approached the parking lot, Trudy noticed her supervisor, Colleen, leaving the building. "Shit, let me run ahead. I know Diane is waiting to go on break and she loves when I'm late so she can complain about having to wait around."

Maxine checked her watch, "It's not even one yet, you've got like five minutes."

"I know, but these bitches are evil and I don't wanna hear shit, so I'm just gonna go. Catch up with ya'll later," Trudy gave a wave of her hand and speed walked toward the office entrance.

Shanae shook her head, "That's a fucked up department, data processing. So glad I don't have to deal with that mess. "

"For real," Maxine responded. As was their usual routine after lunch, they proceeded to walk off their food by strolling around the parking lot once. The loading dock came into view as they turned the bend and two New Rochelle squad cars commanded the attention of the women.

Squinting from the sun, Shanae was able to make out Tonya, the warehouse manager speaking with an officer as he filled out paperwork. "What the hell is going on here?" Shanae asked Maxine as they continued past the dock.

"I don't know but there goes Ben, let's ask him." Maxine started walking toward the warehouse picker as he smoked a cigarette against a tree.

"Hey Ben," Maxine said as they got within earshot.

"Hello ladies, you're looking fine today as always," Ben said smiling his snaggletooth smile. His leathery skin gave him the appearance of someone far older than forty-seven years. Many summers of taking in the sun as a surfer in his youth were to blame for that, but at least he still had all his hair. And it was still blonde to boot.

Shanae graced him with a smile. She genuinely liked Ben; he was always polite and helpful. "Hey, what's up with all the police activity?"

Ben waved his hand dismissively, "Please, damn kids have nothing better to do than ruin people's property. They come here, bring their beer, firecrackers, and drugs no doubt, graffiti the place, and start bonfires. Look at the concrete. Look at the dumpster."

Shanae and Maxine looked and saw black burn marks on the concrete. The dumpster was riddled with graffiti.

"And this isn't the first time," Ben added.

Shanae thought for a minute. Her eyes went from the ground to the top of the loading dock. She started shaking her head slowly and it became rapid as she voiced, "Wait a minute, didn't they catch them on camera?"

"Camera? Man, they haven't had those connected since the renovation."

Shanae thought she misheard him, "What do you mean?" She glanced at Maxine who wanted to hear the answer as much as Shanae.

Ben took a final drag from his cigarette and stomped out the butt before replying. "I'm not exactly sure, but what I heard was, there was a part needed for all of the cameras to sync to a main portal and at the time they couldn't figure it out. As far as I know, the indoor surveillance is all good, but they ran into problems with the exterior set up. You know, he had George doing everything, but George is not a surveillance technician. Mr. Hoffman was supposed to have a technician complete the set up, but never did. All the equipment is in place, it just needs to be connected behind the scenes."

You could have knocked Shanae over with a feather. She was speechless.

Maxine couldn't believe it herself, so she needed clarification. She tried to play it off, "Wow, so Mr. Hoffman's gonna have to get that fixed if he wants this vandalism to stop. Next thing you know they'll be breaking in, and with no cameras we're practically inviting them in," she said looking at Ben.

"My point exactly." Tonya finally called the cops because at least that way we have it documented."

Ben noticed Tonya waving him over and he politely excused himself.

"Can you believe that shit?" Shanae said as they started toward the main entrance.

"That's crazy, but you know what that means right?"

"The fuck I do! That motherfucka Tim obviously don't know that lil' bit of info, huh? Ooh, I'm buggin' right now!" Shanae was beside herself.

"Listen, keep that shit to yourself. We're gonna have to come up with a plan to get the asshole back. He really think he got the upper hand. You better handle this, Shay."

Maxine couldn't stand Timothy and was disgusted that he was using her friend. If there was any way for her to help Shanae get revenge on him, she would. As she entered the building, Shanae's mind was consumed with thoughts of revenge. Timothy was gonna pay, and pay dearly.

ENGLISH RULER

Chapter 7

Facebook became Lowell's new guilty pleasure. He was amazed at the multitude of people he was able to locate; old schoolmates, co-workers, military buddies, the list went on. The big kick was perusing their photos and seeing all that they'd been up to in the years since he last saw them.

One profile in particular caught his attention, that of Jerry Williams. Jerry and Lowell dated best friends in high school, and although Lowell and his girlfriend at the time broke up, apparently Jerry and Danicka married and had a baby. According to Jerry's "About" section of his Facebook page, he was divorced, had two children, and worked in construction.

Although Lowell and Jerry weren't particularity close, they became familiar with each other through many double dates and extracurricular activities due to their girlfriends' friendship. When Lowell broke off his relationship to pursue the military, he didn't keep in touch with Jerry or anyone else from school for that matter. It wasn't that he was turning his back on where he came from; he just wanted to leave the negativity of his old neighborhood and schoolmates behind.

Lowell had sent Jerry a private message and they attempted to fill in the gaps of their time apart. The inbox messages were quickly upgraded to phone calls and the two men realized they had more in common as adults than they did in school. Jerry now lived in Connecticut, as did his ex, Danicka. He was pleasantly surprised with his and Lowell's reconnection and thought his upcoming Memorial Day barbecue would be a great opportunity to catch up in person. Jerry informed Lowell that Danicka would be dropping off their daughter at the event.

"Yo man, I'm pretty sure Melanie is gonna be there too. Her daughter Rhianne and my little Damaris are hip to hip. You haven't mentioned anything, but as far as I remember, you and Mel didn't part on good terms. I'm just giving you the heads up there's a good chance she'll be passing through."

"Yeah, things were pretty strained during our last encounter, but we're all grown now. I'm sure we'll be civil," Lowell tried to sound confident although he was nervous already and her name was only spoken.

Melanie Alexander and Lowell dated all throughout their junior and senior years of high school. Over ten years had passed since he walked out of her life to pursue the military. The breakup was Lowell's choice alone; Melanie was confident that she'd be able to handle a long distance relationship while Lowell didn't give her the option. It was quite a nasty breakup because Melanie was caught off guard. Lowell never withheld his intention of going into the service; it was that he suddenly ended the relationship, crushing Melanie. She was prepared to do the long distance relationship thing. Her love for Lowell was concrete, and she was willing to face the struggles that that type of relationship would present. Unfortunately, she was not given the opportunity.

Lowell went off to the service, eventually being discharged and embarking on a relationship with Giselle. Melanie attended Stony Brook University, earned a Bachelor's degree in Physical Therapy, and began practicing in the area of outpatient orthopedic therapy. Finding herself drawn to sports rehabilitation, she went back to school and earned her Doctorate in Physical therapy with an emphasis in sports medicine. She was successful in her career as a licensed board certified Physical Therapist. Lowell listened quietly as Jerry filled him in on this information.

"She's actually Melanie Robinson now. Her husband is cool; he's a cop though so I don't try to get too close, nah mean?"

"Yeah I feel you on that," Lowell responded.

"So the barbeque starts at three and we usually just go until whenever. And there'll be lots of food and drinks, so feel free to bring guests."

Lowell knew Giselle's mom, Ms. Mabel, was having a cookout as was Patrick and Suzie. Giselle would be helping her mother with the cooking and preparation from early in the morning and then swinging by Patrick's to drop off the kids. He doubted she would want to drive with him to Connecticut as her mom was depending on her.

"Yeah, I'm definitely gonna come through, not sure about my lady though. Her mom is having a barbecue too, and I know she has to help with that."

"Ok cool. So I'll text you the address. Hit me up if anything."

"Cool."

Lowell sat immobile for about ten minutes after the call was disconnected. He was excited and scared at the same time. The reunion between him and Melanie would be an awkward one for sure. But it was laying eyes on Rhianne that could possibly make him become emotional. He and Melanie had talked about starting a family many times during their relationship. Now here she was a mom and he had yet to celebrate his first Father's Day.

Giselle's presence jarred Lowell from his wandering thoughts. She appeared in the bedroom doorway, her auburn tinted micro braids up in a bun, with two loose strands grazing her shoulders. A laundry basket balanced on her hip.

"Hey hun, what are you up to?" she asked, dumping a basket load of clean clothes on the bed. She took notice of the cordless phone in his hand and the unreadable look on his face. Lowell smiled a crooked smile and crossed arms over his chest.

"I got in touch with an old school mate on Facebook and he wants to meet up at his house on Memorial Day for a barbeque."

Giselle laughed, "Oh, so I see Nicola turned you out on Facebook after all."

Smirking Lowell replied, "Not really, I don't think I use it more than the average person."

"See there you go making excuses, the first step is admitting it, you know." They shared laugh and Lowell displayed his domestic side by helping Giselle fold and put away the clean clothes. As he moved around the room, she admired the way his cotton polo hugged his biceps and thought about how lucky she was to have a strong able-bodied companion.

"How've you been feeling lately?"

"Definitely more balanced since taking the insulin. My next appointment is about a week and a half away. Dr. Garcia will check all my levels again and let me know how everything looks on his end."

"Well you feel good, so that's definitely a plus."

"For real."

ENGLISH RULER

£

Two hours later Giselle mingled with fellow parents in the crowded auditorium of White Plains High School. Nicola and the rest of the Flo dance team had just performed an intense routine and were now spread out speaking to students of the school; encouraging them to take up dance. Giselle watched from afar, as Nicola spoke passionately to a young girl no older than eleven.

"Do you like watching music videos and wish you knew all the dances?" Nicola asked the bright eyed cutie in front of her.

The little girl looked at Nicola with awe. She had already thought Nicola was pretty and danced really well, but now that she was speaking with her up, close, and personal, she was further impressed by Nicola's genuine interest and knowledge of all things dance.

"Yeah, I try sometimes, but I never think I can learn the moves or keep up," the young girl responded timidly. "Like the ones you just did up there to Chris Brown's 'Yeah 3Times', do you think I could learn that?" she continued incredulously.

Nicola laughed. Something about the girl in front of her really warmed her spirit and she took an instant liking to her. Nicola placed her arm around the girl's shoulders and steered her toward the summer dance program sign-up table. "Come with me. You're gonna see that you can do anything you put your mind to. Dancing is good for so many reasons; it's a form of expression, it's a form of exercise, and last but not least it's fun. You'll love it."

Ms. Kiara was pleased at the turn out for the dance awareness event. She looked over the logs and saw that so far they had recruited twelve girls for the program. Her goal was to get a few boys involved and make the group a little more diverse, but she was content with the results nonetheless.

Scanning the crowd, she made out several of her current students expertly recruiting new talent; Jadaine was on the stage demonstrating some basic moves for a few students, Tonshea had the attention of some parents as she animatedly explained what the program entailed, two other dancers were at the table physically signing girls up, and Nicola was helping a girl learn how to perform a jazz square.

Ms. Kiara studied Nicola's form and smiled to herself. She knew Nicola was an excellent performer, in addition, she was very patient and understood what it took to show younger students the sometimes difficult dance moves. Nicola had the girl's full attention and Ms. Kiara decided right there that she would pair them together for the season. I can see Nicola mold that child into a graceful swan on the dance floor. Then I'll have a star pupil on both dance tiers, she thought.

Chapter 8

The warm morning sun rays filtered through the mini blinds and beamed across Shanae's queen size bed. Pillow clutched firmly beneath her, left leg lazily hanging off the mattress, sleep completely enveloped her and she was enjoying her comatose state immensely.

Let her tell it, she was at the County Fair hot and just a tad sweaty, waiting in line for the dragon coaster. A light breeze tickled her skin, a welcome relief to the intense heat the sun was emitting. The place was packed and it seemed everyone's thoughts were in sync to take advantage of the warm weather with a day of fun. The scent of popcorn and fried dough filled the air, screams of excitement and laughter could be heard throughout the park, and the various game booths were giving off wacky sounds as they alerted lucky winners.

Shanae took all the activity in as she inched forward in line every few minutes. She usually had Rhianne or a friend with her when she visited the park, but today she appeared to be by her lonesome. When she realized this fact, the line started to move again and her attention was averted to the coaster cars that were filling up rapidly.

Reaching the front of the line, Shanae was stopped by the ride attendant who told her that he needed a party of two to completely fill up the last car. Since she was by herself, he asked her to step aside as he called for a party of two to step to the front of the line.

Within a few seconds, a handsome, strapping man glided toward the attendant with a little girl in tow. He strode past Shanae, tightly holding onto the child's hand, excusing himself as he passed. The little girl smiled at Shanae and she returned the gesture.

Once they were strapped into their seats, the attendant awaited clearance from his counterpart before starting the ride. Shanae watched expectantly as the dragon coaster chugged up the incline pausing dramatically before plunging one hundred and fifty feet, and continuing in a brief journey of twists and turns resulting in ear piercing screams from riders and spectators alike. When the eighty-four second thrill was over, passengers disembarked slightly dizzy, the rush of adrenaline evident on a majority of their faces. Prepared for her turn on the scream machine, Shanae placed her shades in her pocket and got ready to select a seat.

To her disappointment, the ride attendant announced that they had to close the ride for safety checks before allowing the coaster back in operation. The patrons waiting in line voiced their disappointment blatantly, some straight up disrespecting the attendant as if he were personally responsible for their misfortune.

Shanae slowly walked away from the ride, dumbfounded at what had just taken place. How could it be that she waited in line for so long only to have the attendant put a couple ahead of her, then turn around and close the ride before she could indulge? Highly annoyed and somewhat confused, a tug on her shirt caused her to turn around. There stood the same little girl who got on the ride before her; Shanae smiled, curious to know what the girl needed.

Before she could utter a word, "You weren't ready for that ride anyway," spewed from the child's lips. Just as quickly as she appeared, she retreated leaving Shanae dumbfounded.

What the hell... was the only clear thought that ran through Shanae's mind. "Now ain't that some shit!" she said to herself. Standing in the park, the scenery began to spin in a swirl. A psychedelic mix of colors swarmed about her as the words 'Now ain't that some shit' echoed in her head. Faster and faster everything around her became a kaleidoscope of red, orange, blue, green, yellow, and then ultimately it all went black.

Shanae's eyes could not lock in on an image, but her ears were working perfectly. Fuck you and uh, fuck him too, said if I was richer I'd still be witcha, Now ain't that some shit (ain't that some shit)...

In an instant, reality found its way to her mind and she willed her eyes to open. The brightness of the morning sun caused them to involuntarily snap shut once again, but her right hand landed on the bedside table to respond to the annoying sound of Cee Low Green. Her 'Fuck You' ringtone was silenced and she brought the receiver to her ear.

"Hello." Barely above a whisper her voice was heavy with sleep.

"Girl, you better get up. You know we have things to do, plans to make, and hearts to break. Chop, chop!" Maxine was full of life at what Shanae's cable box confirmed was only 8:43am.

"Ugh, mmmm, ok I'm getting up. What's the plan for today?"

"I figure we grab breakfast at IHOP and then hit up the nail salon for some mani-pedis and then get our game plan together because you know Timothy has got to get his." Maxine was hype and ready to initiate payback on behalf of her friend.

"I'm down for that, my nails look like trash. You can come scoop me up since you're all bright eyed and bushy tailed. I'ma jump in the shower and get dressed; I should be ready by the time you get here." Shanae glanced across her bed. "Sweet, see you in a few."

Just as she was pulling the phone away from her ear, Maxine swore she heard the first few bars of Floydd B's 'Luscious' in the distance of Shanae's background; the call was disconnected before she could be sure. She immediately felt uneasy. The only person she knew to have access to the up-and-coming underground artist's tracks was Quincy, Floydd B's cousin and biggest supporter.

None of Floydd's music was widely available and the only time she'd ever head his music was when Quincy played it either in his car or on his cell. He'd even set a few tracks as ringtones. Maxine brushed her hair into a ponytail and hurried around her apartment with the goal of getting to Shanae's as soon as possible; she had a nagging fear to put to rest.

£

Shanae quickly silenced the unexpected ringing and tossed the cell at Quincy, hitting him in the head as she strode toward the bedroom door, "Get up, you gotta leave." A growl escaped his lips at the same time he raised both arms above his head in a serious stretch, "Morning to you, too. What's your problem?"

"Maxine is on her way to pick me up and if you don't get your ass outta here now, we're both gonna have problems!" she stated matter-of-factly and then added, "And you should know when you're over here you gotta silence your fuckin' phone. Got the shit going off all crazy." She left him in the room to take a quick shower.

When she returned he was fully clothed and had his turn in the bathroom as she speed-dressed. Shanae wasted no time hustling Quincy out the door; the last thing she needed was for him to be seen leaving her house – especially by Maxine.

On her way back upstairs, she ran into Jay who was about to prepare breakfast in the tiny kitchen they shared. "Hey Miss Shanae, how you doin' this mornin'?"

"I'm good Jay, what's up with you?"

"I figured you were good having had that fine specimen of a man leave your room this morning. Did you have a good night?" Jay chuckled at his innuendo.

Shanae rolled her eyes and pursed her lips, "You need to stop. Don't you have a man?"

"And?" Jay stuck out his neck and put his hand on his hip matching her attitude.

"You'se a mess, I'll talk to you later."

"Later, Miss Hot-in-the-behind!" Jay really liked Shanae. He was well aware of her promiscuous ways and always made fun of her male visitors. With that said, he was hopeful that one day she would settle down with a good man. From what he saw, she was not a bad person at all. A little confused maybe, but she definitely had a good heart and deserved more than she allowed herself to have.

Shanae reached back to her room just in time hear the bell ring. She parted the blinds and looked out to see Maxine's Hyundai double parked. Ding Dong! "Coming Max, you just rang five seconds ago, damn," she muttered under her breath. When she swung open the door, Maxine nearly knocked her down trying to pass her and get upstairs.

"Why you rolling up in me like that, son? I'm ready to go." Shanae made light of the situation.

"I gotta pee, let me use your bathroom," Maxine yelled behind her, taking the steps two at a time. Since she knew where the bathroom was, Shanae decided to wait for her at the front door. When she was finished, Maxine said from the top of the stairwell, "Shay, come here a minute."

Shanae sucked her breath in and went to the bottom step, "Wassup?"

"I need one of those things, please." Maxine mouthed. "I have my period." She said it just in case Yesenia or Jay could hear her from their rooms.

"Oh, of course."

Maxine didn't have her period much less have to use the bathroom. She was doing a little investigating to settle her fears about what she believed she heard on the phone. Taking note of everything from smell to the state of Shanae's room, specifically the bed, Maxine entered her friend's bedroom. In the short time it took Shanae to retrieve a pad, Maxine had scanned everything within view. She took the pad that was handed to her and returned to the bathroom to keep up her ruse. She didn't find any evidence of Quincy being there and felt foolish for doubting her friend. Still, her intuition told her something was amiss.

£

IHOP in Pelham, NY was one of the restaurant chain's smaller locations but stayed busy nonetheless, being the only one of its kind in the immediate vicinity. Finding the popular breakfast haunt anything but packed was a rare occurrence, so when Maxine pulled her Sonata into the last available parking space in the lot, she felt a sense of triumph. She and Shanae were excited to be immediately ushered to a small booth toward the back of the dining area.

Over pancakes, scrambled eggs, hash browns, bacon, coffee, and fresh squeezed orange juice, the two friends discussed the dilemma with Timothy. It was already established that the external surveillance was nonexistent, but they would need to get confirmation on the internal cameras if they wanted to maximize the opportunity.

"I'm gonna casually bring the cameras up in conversation to Chrissy 'cause if anyone knows about them it's her. She'll know whether or not she paid for the complete interior connection. Finding that out will be easy."

"All right, that's good. So which way do you wanna go with this? You can just end it knowing he can't prove your deal with the vacuums, but knowing you, you're gonna take it to another level." Maxine sipped her coffee. She was ready to help Shanae because in her opinion it was past due for Tim to be put in his place.

"Hell fuckin' yeah! That muthafucka's gonna pay. I still can't believe he contacted Tremaine. He did way too much, all for the sake of getting some ass. So rest assured he will be getting his. I've thought about it, since he loves being daring and having sex in the office, I'm gonna set his ass up lovely."

"What do you have in mind?"

"The ultimate revenge."

"Huh?"

"Check it, he's mad freaky, loves role playing, dressing up, all that shit. What he loves so much will eventually become his downfall. Remember I told you that! When it's all said and done, Tim will not only be unemployed, but he will be ducking rape charges too," Shanae explained triumphantly.

"Ah damn you goin' in,"

"Damn skippy, shit I ain't playin' with his ass. He done fucked me one too many times." Shanae concluded her statement, they both looked at each other and chuckled at the double meaning albeit, laughter was only an option because revenge was in motion.

Several coffee refills later, they were satisfied with the plan they painstakingly crafted. All the details had been fine tuned and all that was left was to put the plan into motion. Shanae was the main player, but Maxine would need to keep her eyes and ears open as well as have the correct things to say if it came to it.

After their run at IHOP, they headed toward Grace Nails on Fourth Avenue in Mt. Vernon with beautification on their minds. Grace Nail Salon was the most popular nail salon in the city, and both Maxine and Shanae had trusted their nails to Grace for years.

When they entered the salon, they knew they were lucky to have reached when they did; the place was filling up quickly. Salon Owner Grace Yeong appeared and greeted them warmly voicing her usual line, "Long time you no come eeh." It could have been two days and Grace would have said the same thing. She knew how to keep women coming back to her salon. As the plaque stated above the cash register, there's no such thing as too beautiful, and it was obvious the women (and men) who kept Grace Nails in business certainly believed that. Maxine followed Grace to the back room to have her fake eyelashes redone, while Shanae eased into a massage chair and had her feet tended to by Peter, the best and only male nail technician at Grace's. After a few minutes of sitting there with her eyes closed, enjoying the attention to her feet, Shanae's peace was interrupted.

"Shanae?" Shanae opened her eyes at the sound of the vaguely familiar voice and saw her former neighbor, Lisette, sitting in the chair next to her. Oh great, this gossiping bitch! "Oh, hey Lisette, how've you been?" She responded with a fake smile.

Lisette lived in the apartment two doors over from the one Shanae had shared with Tremaine. She was the single mother of three kids with just as many daddies and was known to get into and reveal everyone's business including her own. For that reason, Shanae minimized their conversations to hi and bye. Regrettably, in her current position she was unable to avoid Lisette's impending barrage of questions.

"I'm good, girl. How have you been? I didn't even know you weren't staying on 7th anymore. I seen Tremaine the other day and asked him about you. He told me ya'll broke up," Lisette said, trying to sound like a concerned friend.

No this bitch is not looking at me like I owe her an explanation. She needs to be somewhere taking some birth control, not worrying about who I'm with. "Yeah, it's been a few weeks now." Shanae left it at that.

"I was like; I know he didn't cheat on her. Men can be such dogs sometimes," Lisette continued to pry. Shanae just gave her a plastered on smile. When she saw that Shanae wasn't going to reveal any details, Lisette went for the jugular. "I saw this chic leaving his house the other morning. She said 'hi' to me, but I didn't keep a conversation with her."

Yeah Right. Not with the way you run your mouth. "That's cool, we both have to move on and live our lives, you know what I mean." Not only did she not care, she didn't believe Lisette. She figured she was just fishing to get info to approach Tremaine herself. The way she used to look at him when they all lived in the building was not lost on Shanae. Shanae had no worries because she already had one up on her.

"Yes I do," Lisette replied and tried to nonchalantly scope Shanae out from head to toe. This was not lost on Shanae who thanked her lucky stars that she always took the time to look presentable. Today she wore black denim capris, a racerback--

silver and white tunic with matching jewelry for Lisette's viewing pleasure. 'You never know who you'll run into' was her motto.

That was more than she could say for Lisette whose oval-shaped face was covered in a foundation that was a couple of shades too light. Her skin tight jeans fit her a little too snug to be considered sexy, and her one shouldered blouse appeared tacky rather than seductive. She was definitely trying, but she was not Tremaine's type and Shanae knew it. She smiled to herself and then muffled a sigh of relief when she saw Maxine heading her way.

"Grace wants you in the wax room for your brows before you get polished." Thankful for the rescue, Shanae looked at Peter who was now massaging lotion into her legs. He tapped her legs and said, "Ok, ok. When finished, you pick color. I polish."

"Ok girl, you take care," Shanae said, easing out of her seat.

"All right Shanae, it was good seeing you."

"You too," was Shanae's reply although she secretly hoped Lisette was gone by the time she returned. Never fails. Every time I come on Fourth Ave I gotta see someone I know. Madness!

Chapter 9

Memorial Day weekend was off to a hot and muggy start. At eleven o'clock in the morning, the temperature was already pushing ninety degrees and the air quality was unforgiving. Lowell loved the hot weather, but even he was skeptical about how they would fare being outside all day.

With Nicola and Marcelle at Patrick's house, he and Giselle spent most of the morning in the Bronx at her mom's house helping prepare for the barbecue later that day. Although Giselle was busy in the kitchen prepping all types of culinary delights, Lowell didn't partake and chose instead to stay busy with the tent and grill set up. A couple of Giselle's family members had arrived early to lend a hand and progress was taking shape.

When the tent was up and the grills were fired up, Lowell took a breather. He was developing a mild headache and realized it had been several hours since he'd had something to eat. He entered the kitchen and caught Ms. Mabel taste testing the potato salad.

"Caught," he laughed.

Giselle's fifty-something mother turned around slowly, mouth full of salad, "You ain't right. You know Giselle's potato salad is my weakness."

Lowell laughed. He got along very well with Ms. Mabel and thought the world of her. "That's ok, I think I'll have some as well," he said, grabbing a paper plate and scooping on a few spoons of the salad. He lifted tin foil off a pan and snatched two hot wings to add to his plate. Ms. Mabel laughed. She knew if Giselle saw him disrupting her dish, he would get a smack on the hand. Taking his food outside, he saw Giselle and her cousin, Marissa, inspecting his handiwork. "Is it done to your liking ladies?"

Marissa was the first to answer, "Barely passable Mr. Washington however, I'll let it slide this time."

Lowell just smiled and shook his head. Although Marissa was five years Giselle's junior, the two women were very close. Lowell took a liking to Marissa because she was a free spirit and had a positive attitude, not to mention she was a joker like him.

"Well lucky for me," he responded with a grin.

Marissa stuck out her tongue and walked away.

"What's up hun?" Giselle noticed he looked a little winded.

"Ah, nothing. I felt a headache coming on, so I'm just eating a little something."

Giselle's thoughts immediately went to his diabetes. "Did you take your insulin last night?"

"Yup."

Worry covered her face, "Low, you know with your health condition you have to be eating right and taking care of yourself. I can't afford for anything to happen to you." She grabbed his hand, as she looked him in the eyes. "I'm not playing about having a baby; I'm ready so you've got to be doing the right thing."

"Okay, Spike Lee." Lowell joked about it but he knew the seriousness of her tone. He was content that he was at least taking the steps to address the issues of his past. It was clear to him that he had to take care of that ASAP, especially with Giselle pressuring him to have a baby. He looked around the yard and then checked his watch.

"You getting ready to go to Connecticut?"

"Yeah, I figure it'll take close to two hours to get to Hartford from here so if I leave now, I'll arrive at about four or so. His barbecue started at twelve, so that's a good time to arrive."

"All right. Well, I bought a case of Heineken for you to take with you. It's in the foyer. Don't forget it."

"Thanks babe. Let me go say bye to your mom." Lowell gave Giselle a peck on the lips and started toward the house just as someone turned on the stereo system. Seemed Ms. Mabel's barbecue was just getting underway.

HOEISM: BORNTODOIT

£

The entire drive to Connecticut, Lowell was playing out scenes in his head. He had no idea how Melanie would react to seeing him after all these years, or how he was going to react to seeing her for that matter. He tried to keep a positive outlook and stay calm as he cruised just above the speed limit on I-95.

He reached East Hartford in good time and as he turned on Jerry's block, he heard the funky beats of Flo Rida's 'Good Feeling' blaring. He quickly found a spot to park, grabbed the case of beer, and strolled to the small one family home where the music was coming from, double checking the house number to ensure he was at the right place.

Lowell smiled and greeted the few adults hanging out on the front porch and followed the pathway to what turned out to be a generously sized backyard. There was a semi-in ground pool to the far left, dual barbecue pit to the right, and a large canopy with tables and chairs decorated with the festive red, white, and blue colors in the center.

Toward the very rear of the yard was a large trampoline with a netting enclosure; several kids were taking advantage of its presence. People were milling about, some dancing, others eating or drinking Most of the kids were enjoying the pool; a few were running around with super soakers. There was even a DJ in one corner with a full laptop and mixer setup. Lowell was feeling the vibe. If Melanie was there, she was not within his view. He hoped he got there before her, somehow that eased his mind a little, although she was better friends with Jerry than he was.

He scanned the area for Jerry and turned his attention toward the back steps when he heard a screen door bang shut. There, descending the steps with a pan of raw, seasoned chicken was Jerry Williams. He was in full griller's garb with a spatula sticking out of his 'License to Grill' apron and chef's hat perched on his head. Lowell's lips turned up at the sides to reveal his near-pearly whites as he sauntered toward his old friend. Jerry lowered the pan onto a table and looked up to a grinning Lowell.

"My man! You made it." Jerry and Lowell clasped palms and did the brother-man hug thing.

"Of course, how could I not?" Lowell was actually happy to see Jerry. It gave him a sense of nostalgia and memories of his days at Mt. Vernon High School came flooding back.

"Did you find the place okay? It's pretty much a straight drive."

"Yeah the drive was fine. Hey I brought a few bottles to add to the bar," Lowell said displaying the case of beer.

"Good looking, do me a favor and empty that into the red cooler over there next to the bench."

"A'ight." Lowell walked over, emptied the case and placed the flattened box in the garbage. Jerry was putting a fresh batch of chicken on the grill when he returned.

"This is a really nice place you have here," Lowell said, surveying the property. "Thanks again for the invite."

"You're welcome over anytime. It's just me. Damaris is here every other weekend and sometimes my niece or Mel's daughter comes over to keep her company. The first Friday night of every month I host a spades night."

"Spades? What you know about spades?" Lowell joked.

"Negro please, I will take you in spades any day. Matter of fact, bring your butt down here for next month's games and I'll rip you a new one."

Lowell nodded as he said, "I just may take you up on that."

The men chatted for a few moments longer until Lowell felt compelled to ask, "So where is your little girl?" What he really wanted to ask was, "So where's Melanie and her daughter?" but he settled for the former.

"Ah my bad, let me introduce you to my princess. Come." Jerry guided Lowell over to the pool, pausing to chat with a few guests along the way. They stepped up onto the surrounding deck and Jerry walked over to a table of kids playing Uno. There were three girls and two boys and all looked up as the men approached. "Damaris come here for a sec, I want you to meet my friend," Jerry said to a pint-sized version of himself.

The girl pushed herself away from the table and walked over to her dad with a multi-colored towel wrapped around her waist. Her tie-dyed bathing suit was secured around her neck, and her damp hair dripped droplets of water onto her shoulders.

"This is my friend, Lowell. We went to school together. Lowell, this is my daughter, Damaris."

"Hello Damaris, nice to meet you." Lowell offered her his hand to shake and noticed that even though she looked a lot like Jerry, she had Danicka's dark, curly hair.

"Nice to meet you too," Damaris replied smiling wide enough to display a gap where one of her front teeth should have been. "So, was my dad good in school?" Damaris was smiling but Jerry knew his child was serious.

Lowell laughed aloud then snuck a quick look at Jerry, "Yeah, he was okay."

"Okay? Just okay? What does that mean," Jerry faked annoyance.

"No, for real, he was a good kid."

"Thank you, sheez. Who do I have to pay to support my stellar reputation?"

"Daddy, you're not famous, you don't have a reputation!" Damaris scrunched her eyebrows as she looked at her father for an explanation.

Lowell nearly keeled over trying to hold in his laughter. He crossed his arms and studied what was sure to be a comical father/daughter exchange. Jerry looked at Lowell incredulously, who in return shrugged and gave a look like 'this one's all you bruh.' Jerry turned to answer Damaris and noticed Danicka approaching them from the side of the house.

"We'll talk about my reputation later, here comes your mom, let's see what she wants."

Seconds later Danicka was upon them, winded and slightly flustered. She barely glanced at Lowell and offered a brief "hi" before turning to Jerry. "The beer and ice are in the car. Can you ask one of your nephews to take them out for me? I need to get something to drink and cool off, I feel like I'm gonna pass out," she handed him the car keys and used a napkin to dab the sweat that dotted her forehead and upper lip.

"Yeah, I got it, don't worry," he looked to Damaris. "Go with your mom and make sure she gets something to drink."

"And you know you can hang out inside in the air conditioning if you want," he said to Danicka, although he knew she wouldn't.

"Thanks," Danicka said over her shoulder as she and Damaris retreated. It wasn't lost on Lowell that Jerry allowed his gaze to settle on her denim covered behind as she left.

"Come help me grab these things out the car real quick, Lowell," Jerry removed his apron.

"Yeah, of course."

The men started toward the front yard. Jerry paused at a group of men laughing and drinking beer at the side of the house. "Mike, man the grill for me a sec, I've gotta grab a few things."

"Man, don't be too long. You know a brother can't cook," replied the lanky teen. He took the apron and hat that were handed to him and subconsciously pulled up his sagging jeans.

"Burn my food and we're gonna have problems. I'll be right back."

When they reached a white SUV in the driveway, Jerry deactivated the alarm and popped the trunk. "So I take it Danicka didn't recognize me. You did tell her I was coming, right?" Lowell knew Melanie was nearby, from what Jerry had told him in their conversations, she and Danicka were still inseparable.

"Actually, I didn't. Me and Danicka are not together anymore and I don't have to report my guests to her. But trust me, once she takes a good look at you, she'll know who you are. You nervous?" Jerry stacked two cases of beer while Lowell grabbed the bags of ice.

Lowell shrugged. "I guess you could say that." The men started toward the house.

"Well it's too late because there she is walking to the backyard as we speak."

Lowell whipped his head to the left and saw a figure in a tan dress bending the corner. His heart rate sped up. He didn't need to see her face to know it was Mel; she had the same swagger.

He followed Jerry through the front door and into his modest but well-kept home. The air conditioned living room provided temporary relief from the sweltering sun and the two men decided to enjoy a cold beer before going back out into the heat.

A few of Jerry's family members were back and forth shuttling food and supplies to and from the yard. Jerry was enjoying Lowell's company and wanted him to feel comfortable, so he made sure to introduce him to his family and friends as they passed through. When they had a brief moment alone, Lowell asked quietly, "So about Mel, she came with Danicka or what?"

"Nah, I see Mel's truck outside so she drove herself. But they'll most likely leave together though. Danicka doesn't stay at my parties, she'll drop my daughter off, maybe have a drink or two, and then she's out." Jerry brought the Heineken bottle to his lips and bent his head back to finish the last of his lager. Lowell followed suit. He didn't come all this way to see Melanie from afar. He needed to see her face to face, talk to her, explain things.

"A'ight let me make my appearance before she leaves then," Lowell was fresh off a splash of liquid courage, but surely required something stronger to settle the nerves that were on edge.

Jerry patted his friend on the back and led him out through the backdoor. The DJ had switched to a popular reggae selection, and everyone, kids and adults alike, were getting their dance on. As they made their way across the yard, Jerry saw Danicka swaying her hips to the beat; apparently, she had cooled off. Right next to her was Melanie, moving fluidly to the sounds, nursing a wine cooler. Jerry led Lowell right up to the women and there was no time for them to prepare themselves for the sudden intrusion.

"You alright now?" Jerry asked Danicka.

She nodded, "Thanks."

"No prob," he turned his attention to Melanie.

"Hey Mel, you didn't even let me know you were here," Jerry said greeting her with a kiss on the cheek.

"What's up? I just got here a little while ago with Danicka. I was expecting to see you manning the grill as usual," Melanie was still well into the music and doing a two-step as she spoke. Her tan strapless dress hit her just above the knees, the bottom ruffles flirting with the wind with every move she made. The wide chocolate colored belt accentuated her tiny waist and matched the gladiator sandals that showed off her pedicure, and wrapped around her ankles.

Lowell quietly scoped her out while she spoke with Jerry and he appreciated her attention to detail. He noticed her nails were well manicured and the costume jewelry she wore complimented her outfit beautifully. Her oversized shades were perched atop her head, holding her natural locks back from her face. The DJ began to mix in Sean Kingston's 'Fire Burning' when Jerry grabbed Lowell's shoulder and said, "Look who stopped by."

At this point, both Melanie and Danicka were forced to acknowledge the man that was being presented to them.

Melanie had taken notice of the man standing there, but now took a concentrated look at him. Smiling expectantly, she met his gaze and fleetingly scanned his lean frame, stealing a glance at his low haircut, buff chest, and then back to meet his warm eyes. Those eyes!

There was something familiar about them and when he greeted her with, "Hey, how've you been?" She just knew her mind was playing tricks on her. She hadn't heard that voice in years and never thought she would again. She was momentarily speechless, but the frozen smile on her face provided some form of social acknowledgement at the very least.

Danicka finally recognized him and wasted no time letting him know it, "Lowell?" she asked disbelievingly.

Lowell smiled sheepishly, "How are you Danicka? I saw you earlier but you didn't seem to be feeling well."

"I'm fine, thank you. The heat got to me is all. Give me a hug. Oh my gosh, how long has it been?" she asked, opening her arms wide.

"Almost eleven years. I left for the military in 2001," he engulfed her in his embrace and was relieved she was so inviting.

"Well that explains all that muscle your packing," she joked as she squeezed his taut bicep.

Lowell smirked, "It's really great seeing you. It was crazy how I found Jerry on Facebook; everyone has one of those things, huh?"

"You know it. I'm gonna have to add you now, what's your user name?'

"Same ol' Lowell Washington."

"Cool, I'm about to send you a request," Danicka stated, pulling up the Facbook application on her android phone.

"Ah hell no," Jerry voiced looking across his yard in the direction of his prized Weber. Mike looked panicked as tall flames shot up from the grill, threatening to set the borrowed chef hat ablaze. Jerry took off toward the chaos.

Lowell shook his head and turned his attention back to Melanie. "So, how've you been, Mel?"

The reality of her teenage lover standing before her was still sinking in, but Melanie had found her voice. Her heart fluttered when he called her by her nickname. Back in the day, it was very rare for him to call her name in full. "I'm well, thanks. It's a surprise seeing you here." She played with the hem of her dress.

"Yeah as I told Danicka, it's a riot who you can find through Facebook these days."

"Tell me about it."

Silence prevailed as the former lovers tried to look anywhere but into each other's eyes.

"So what have you been up to in the years since I last saw you? Jerry told me you're a physical therapist." Lowell did his best to keep a conversation going. He didn't have a script laid out in his head, but he had to take advantage of this face to face opportunity with the woman whose heart he tore apart years ago.

"Yeah, I got my degree from Stony Brook and then went back and got my doctorate specializing in sports medicine. What about you?" She looked up and met his gaze for a brief moment before looking past him at the children frolicking in the pool.

"Well, as you know I went into the service for several years, I went through the ranks but I'm currently an Aviation Manager for National."

"That's cool."

Melanie wanted to know if he was married, but wouldn't dare ask. His left hand was in his pocket, so she couldn't tell by that either. She bounced slightly to the music as she turned things over in her mind thinking of something appropriate to say.

Danicka had wandered off, no doubt to give the couple a moment alone, but their private moment was abruptly interrupted by two little girls who ran full speed into Melanie. Each girl had grabbed onto a leg, out of breath and overcome with laughter.

"What are you two troublemakers up to?" Melanie asked the twosome.

"Mommy, Kevin's chasing us with a dead snail," said Rhianne, breathing hard.

"Yeah, he's trying to put it down our shirt," continued Damaris, obviously wanting some sort of revenge.

Melanie looked up and saw Kevin duck behind a trash can. She looked back at the girls and said, "Okay, I'll help you deal with Kevin, but first you girls should say hi to my friend, Lowell. You just interrupted our conversation." The two girls looked at Lowell, noticing him for the first time.

Lowell's mouth was dry. He already knew Damaris from their introduction earlier, but he couldn't believe the brown-skinned little beauty in front of him had just referred to Melanie as mom. He fought to keep his composure as he said, "Now I know you Damaris, we met earlier."

"Yup," she said smiling.

"But who's this cutie pie?" he gave Rhianne his full attention.

"This is my best friend Rhianne. Rhianne, this is Lowell, he went to school with my dad and said he was a good kid," Damaris stated matter-of-factly.

Lowell and Melanie laughed at that statement when Rhianne waved her hand in front of her and offered, "Hi Lowell, nice to meet you," she said shyly. Her hair seemed to be Willow Smith inspired being intricately braided up on each side and left to hang in a sort of Mohawk at the right side of her head. With her little denim dress and wrap-around sandals she looked like a mini Melanie.

"Hello Rhianne, how are you?" Lowell tried to commit each of her features to memory. There was so much he wanted to say, so much he wanted to do with her. In time, he hoped to make those things come true.

"I'm good, thanks," Pretty and polite. Melanie's doing a great job. "That's good. Well it was nice meeting you. And if you need help with that Kevin boy and the snail you just let me know," Lowell said trying to come off lighthearted, but he was serious.

"Okay."

"You two go ahead and let me finish talking. I'll be over there in a minute," Melanie instructed. The girls ran off toward the trampoline looking over their shoulders, no doubt for Kevin and the snail.

"She's a cutie pie Melanie, how old is she?"

"Thank you, she's ten and a half," Melanie smiled.

Lowell nodded, thinking to himself. There was another bout of silence before he took an audible deep breath.

"You know Mel, I know it may not be the place or time, but I just need to let you know that I'm sorry for leaving the way I did. And I know there's nothing I can do to change the past, but I feel you deserve to hear that from me face to face," he looked her right in the eyes as he said this. Melanie swallowed and looked away.

"Well you know to be honest, if you were to say this some years ago I'd tell you to go fuck yourself. Time has eased my bitterness and I'm now mature enough to understand that we're allowed to make our own decisions, and I respect you for making yours." Then to ease the tension she added, "No apology needed, we're grown folk now. We learn from our mistakes and we move on, right?"

"Right...umm, so with that said, who's the lucky guy? Yes, I peeped the rock." They both laughed.

"Rock? Hardly. His name is Randy Robinson and he's an officer with the NYPD."

Lowell nodded, "nice, so it's Melanie Robinson now?"

"Alexander-Robinson. I didn't want to get rid of Alexander, mom's death hit me hard and I wanted to keep her name alive."

"I totally understand, and I know it's been a long while, but I am sorry for your loss. Ms. Alexander was a trip," Lowell reminisced.

"She was wasn't she?" Melanie agreed. "I know you remember my Aunt Lorraine."

"Of course, how is she?"

Melanie nodded, "she's great. You know we were always close, but mom's death brought her, Shanae and me even closer. We are the closest thing to her only sister and all."

"I'm sure. Hey how's your sister doing these days?" Tread carefully Low.

"She's okay actually. She still lives in Mt. Vernon and works for a private company in New Rochelle. Marching to the beat of her own drum as usual, ya know?"

Lowell nodded. "That's cool."

"Yeah, you know Shanae, she's still wild but what can I say? That's my only sibling and I love her," Melanie shrugged. She recalled how, as a young teen, Shanae used to get into so much trouble with boys and was just into everything. Being the older sister, she had to look out for her, and often times Lowell was present for the latest fiasco.

Lowell chuckled slightly, "yeah, I know." A rare breeze carried the scent of freshly cooked beef kebabs and burgers that were fresh off the grill straight to Lowell's nostrils. He grabbed and rubbed his stomach to ease the unexpected hunger pang.

"You want to get something to eat? I haven't had anything yet."

Melanie looked around the yard trying to spot Rhianne. "I do, but I should check on Rhianne and make sure Kevin's not still harassing her and Damaris. I'll have to make sure she ate too, so go ahead. Thanks though."

"No problem." Since he had a moment, Lowell decided it was a good time to check his blood sugar. He quietly slipped away from the festivities and sat in his car. From the glove compartment, he retrieved his

One Touch® Ultra Mini and proceeded to check his glucose level. The machine read 54mg/d, which meant he was out of whack. Great excuse to devour one of those thick, juicy burgers I peeped, he thought. He strolled back to the house and washed his hands before joining Jerry at the grill.

"I see you reclaimed your throne," Lowell joked.

Jerry shook his head, "Not sure what I was thinking. Young buck almost burned the place down. What's up with you, I saw nothing but smiles over there between you two."

Lowell nodded purposefully, "It's all good, better than I imagined that's for sure. But we'll talk on that at a later date."

Jerry took Lowell's cue and pretended to crick his neck so he could look over his shoulder. Danicka was approaching. "Hook me up with one of those burgers my stomachs been crying for," Lowell continued.

A broad smile spread across Jerry's face, "Oh you're about taste a piece of heaven and don't say you haven't been warned. Grab a plate."

Lowell did as he was told and eagerly sunk his teeth into the piping hot burger. His taste buds were immediately awakened and his belly was thanking him silently. "I'm gonna need another one of these joints."

Jerry was now smirking, "Told you."

"He told you what? He always wanna be tellin' someone 'I told you so," Danicka chimed in as she reached the men.

"You know I'm the top chef around here Danicka. It's not like I'm lying," Jerry offered, slyly placing his arm around her shoulders.

Danicka moved out of his embrace, "I don't know about all that, but the burgers do look good. Let me get one."

"I always knew you still wanted my meat," Jerry said looking at her sideways.

Lowell busted out laughing.

"You know what…" Danicka crossed her arms and leaned back on her left leg. She took the burger Jerry offered her and swatted him as she walked away.

The solar lights around the property created a relaxing ambiance as the sun made its retreat. The DJ was still spinning the latest hits and everyone seemed to be having a good time. Lowell chatted with Danicka and Melanie some more and was able to get more familiar with Jerry's friends and family. He was secretly elated about several exchanges he had with Rhianne and found her to be extremely bright and well-mannered.

It was eight-fifteen when he checked his watch and decided to prepare for the lonely drive home to

Tarrytown. Walking around the backyard, he took his time saying goodbye to the various people he'd met, making sure not to miss Damaris and Rhianne.

He reached Melanie and Danicka and was surprised to hear Danicka say, "Lowell don't be a stranger, I don't wanna have to e-thug you on Facebook."

"Never that, never that," was his reply. To Melanie he said, "Mel, I can't tell you how good it was to see and talk to you. I'm sorry it took so long. Hopefully we it won't be the last time."

Melanie was feeling nice off the 1800 Select Silver Tequila in her cup and proved to be a little chummier than she normally would've been. She opened up her arms and pulled Lowell close, inhaling his Ralph Lauren cologne. "Lowell I can't believe I'm actually seeing you. We'll talk again, get me as friend from Danicka's page," she said with a heavy tongue. When they pulled away from each other, Lowell did everything to keep the grin from taking over his face, don't have to tell me twice.

On the drive home, Lowell reflected on the day's events and felt content. He'd finally taken the first steps of many to settle his past indiscretions. Today went smoothly and he continued to pray for strength that when all was said and done, he wouldn't find himself a single man.

Chapter 10

"So when're you gonna let me hit it again?" the deep voice said with an air of cockiness.

"Why don't you ask your girl that?" Shanae asked cradling the phone between her left ear and shoulder as she flipped through her mail.

"Stop playin.' I can come by tonight."

"Nicca, you ain't comin' ova here!" Shanae's voice raised an octave and she screwed up her face in displeasure. She straightened her back and got serious taking the phone from the crook of her neck and placing it properly to her ear.

"Why you actin' all brand new, Shanae? You wasn't actin' all high and mighty when I was bangin' your back out!"

Because I can't afford for your nosey-ass girl to be in my business, she thought.

"Listen Keyonne, you're not coming to my house and we ain't getting' down like that no more, ok? Besides you have your wifey—Lisette—why don't you get some from her?"

"Fuck her! She be tryna act tight with the goods. Plus, I told you I'm done with her ass anyway. I don't even be on Seventh checkin' her like that, I just see about my lil' man and break out," Keyonne responded.

"Good, you're supposed to see about your son. You're not up on Seventh like that and I don't live there no more, so let's just do our own thing. Me and you were never a couple and don't owe each other a damn thing." She was losing her patience.

"Since when did you become such a bourgeois bitch? Actin' like you better tha…"

"Wait, so because I ain't givin' you no ass I'm a bourgeois bitch? But just seconds ago it was 'lemme hit that yo.' Get the fuck outta here."

"Whatever, Shananay! You a dick lovin' round-the-way-hoe just like the rest of them," Keyonne eloquently retorted.

"Is that really the best you can do? Come on let's take two and this time give me some emotion."

"You really are a crazy ass bitch."

"Thanks. And remember that the next time you're about to dial my number," Shanae responded without hesitation.

The click and silence she heard next confirmed that she had finally succeeded in getting Keyonne off her phone. She pressed the end button, relieved to be rid of him and his drama. Her mind involuntarily replayed the scene that took place eight months ago when she and Lisette both showed up at Grace Nails for their appointments.

Shanae had just put her hands under the dryer when Lisette walked in with Keyonne. At first, they didn't notice her, and Lisette was behaving normally. But by the time she settled in at the manicurist table she had peeped Shanae and after greeting her, made a big deal about asking Keyonne his opinion on the color and shape of her nails.

After ten minutes of, "Baby, do you think I should do a French or get an airbrush design?" and "Hun, do you think this is a good length?" Shanae was ready to leave before she puked. There was no reason for Lisette, her then neighbor, to behave in such a manner.

It was clear that she was insecure and needed the constant validation of her man in the presence of an attractive woman. Shanae didn't want to be the reason for any woman to come out of their natural character, so she gave her freshly done acrylic tips a spritz of finishing spray, said farewell and left.

No sooner than she walked out the door did Keyonne make his move. He was standing in front of the salon smoking a cigarette and slyly approached her. When she first noticed he was beckoning her, it appeared as though he was picking something off the ground that she had dropped.

"Excuse me Miss, you dropped this," Keyonne had said giving her a brief once-over.

Shanae glanced at the ground and then at his hand. Out of instinct, she took what he handed her. On first glance, it appeared to be a simple Grace Nails business card, but knowing better, she turned it over to reveal the name Keyonne and a phone number.

Leaning against the glass storefront, Keyonne said, "Hit me up, Ma. You sexy as hell." Everything happened so quickly. Shanae looked behind Keyonne, through the window of the salon and saw that Lisette had her back to them. She shook her head at him and stuffed the card into her pocket. Out of curiosity, she dialed those digits the very next day and began what would become a secret but intense booty call relationship. Lisette lived across the street from Shanae and Tremaine at the time and apparently, Keyonne had been scoping her out for weeks. It was his luck to finally have the chance to slip her his number. Now after eight months of lying and sneaking around it was finally over. Seeing Lisette in Grace's and hearing her pry about Tremaine and the break-up shook Shanae. She figured she better put a stop to it before things blew out of proportion. After all, there was still Timothy to deal with. Timothy...

Seeing that all of the mail was outstanding bills, Shanae threw them to the side and ran over the plan to bring Timothy down. She smiled when she thought of how ingenious it all was. Though a little nervous, she was ready. The groundwork had already been laid and the only thing left to do was put it all into motion.

Hunger pains cramped her belly and told her it was time to bust open the small oxtail with rice and peas she had bought earlier from the local Royal Caribbean Bakery. She eased off her bed and padded to the kitchen. Where she found her food was still warm. A glass of iced tea and food in hand, Shanae began to exit the kitchen when she noticed an envelope on the countertop that bore her name. She grabbed it and continued to her room. In the confines of her small, but neatly arranged bedroom Shanae wolfed down the popular West Indian dish and quickly fell asleep with her belly full.

An hour and a half later she was awakened by the sounds of Rhianna crooning about how she fell in love in a hopeless place. It took a minute for her to realize that it was her newly assigned ringtone. When she saw the caller was her aunt Lorraine, she quickly answered.

"Hi Auntie."

"Hey baby, how are you doing?"

"I'm good, just tired."

"Well you sound like you were sleeping."

"Yeah, I just dozed off after having some oxtail from Royal. I forgot how that food really puts me out," Shanae said rubbing her barely there stomach.

"It's not the food, it's you young people. Ya'll don't know how to eat right, always turning to a burger and fries for nourishment. You need to eat like that more often; it makes your back strong," her aunt wisely advised.

Shanae giggled, "You sound like Mommy."

"Good, you know she'd be telling you the same thing."

"I know," Shanae said reflectively.

Changing the subject, her aunt got the real reason for her call.

"So how's everything been going with the room and everything? Are you comfortable?"

"For the most part I am, but I don't wanna get too comfy 'cause I don't plan to stay here that long."

"Well that's good. You gotta get back on your feet, find an apartment and get your confidence back."

Shanae was slightly taken aback by her aunt's comment. "What do you mean 'get my confidence back'?"

Aunt Lorraine chuckled, "Baby girl, you can try fooling yourself by denying the facts, but I know you too well for you to be trying to fool me. Now I seen that Tremaine the other day over by Pathmark and he told me what went down between you two –"

"Auntie…" Shanae was ready to put up a defense.

"Let me finish. You never told me the specifics of your break-up and that's your prerogative, but don't get mad at him. The boy obviously needed to get some things off his chest because that's the longest I've ever held a conversation with him and you two ain't even a couple anymore. He's hurt, but he'll get over it. You on the other hand, always trying to hide things and handle them on your own is gonna be your downfall. You know you can talk to me about anything; I won't judge you. If I can help you, I will. That's what I'm here for. I know things aren't right with you because for one, you've hardly been over to see me since the move. And then Rhianne spent the night the other day and she was telling me you've been lacking in your visits to her as well. Knowing how much you love that child, when I heard that, I knew you were going through something."

Shanae had teared up hearing her aunt speak the truth. "I am, but I'm working on it, I really am," she sniffed.

"Okay. I didn't mean to upset you, but I need you to be aware and not let these things consume you. What you do with your life is your business, but you have to remember the consequences of your actions. Always remember that I love you, baby girl."

"I love you too, Auntie."

"Now don't make me wait too long before I see you again. Next time I'll be making a trip over there instead of a phone call," Aunt Lorraine advised lovingly.

"I won't. I'll be over soon, I promise."

"Alright then, we'll talk."

"Okay, bye."

"Bye, baby."

Relaxing back in her queen sized bed, Shanae thought about what her aunt said, I've gotta get outta this slump and get my shit together. And Tremaine is confiding in Aunt Lorraine…

For a brief moment, Shanae felt a smidgen of remorse for deceiving her former lover but just as quickly, she rationalized that men had been doing the same thing to women for years. Fuck it, it is what it is. Her eyes found their way to the bedside table where the letter she brought in from the kitchen lay. She had forgotten about it but now grew more interested when she realized upon closer inspection, that it bore no postmark and no return address. When flipped over, she saw that it was sealed shut and did not appear to be tampered with.

The plain white legal sized envelope simply said To Shanae across the front center, and it wasn't hand written. Someone took the time to type it out on a P-touch type device and affix the label to the envelope. Using one of her airbrushed acrylic nails, she carefully opened the envelope to reveal a single sheet of white copy paper with two neatly typed sentences: This is not a joke. Leave my man alone or there will be consequences to pay.

Shanae turned the paper over to find the back blank. There was no signature or any other feature to piece together where the letter came from. While most other women would have been even mildly concerned, Shanae wasn't the least bit worried. To her credit, she did mull over who could have known where she lived since her address was relatively new, Quincy comes over all the time, but Maxine would have confronted me, I know that much. Keyonne and Timothy have never been here so I don't think it's either of their women; And none of them know where I live.

She slid her feet into a pair of fuzzy slipper socks and went down the hall to find out which one of her housemates retrieved the letter from the mailbox.

Yesenia's room was silent and there was no light peeking through under the doorjamb; Shanae assumed she wasn't home just yet and continued on to Jay's door.

Banging hard to be heard over a Donna Summer classic, Shanae had to burst out laughing when he opened the door to reveal himself in full drag. A blonde bouffant-style wig atop his head, a multi-colored satin mini dress with matching duster on his average frame, sheer pantyhose covering manly legs, platform high heels on his feet, and make-up that could rival any fashion model completed his ensemble. Using a phrase of the "kids," he was looking fierce!

"And watchu laughin' at, Ms. Thang? It is not a joke that I look better than you, ok!" Jay responded snapping his fingers in her face and bringing his hand to rest on his right hip.

"Yeah, whatever. I've never seen you in full drag before, that's all. This all looks really good. You go all out I see," Shanae said reaching up to touch one of his dangling earrings.

Swatting her hand away, Jay inquired about her presence, "Chile, I already know I'm fabulous, but what else did you want exactly? I have Donna waiting you know."

Shanae rolled her eyes in an exaggerated manner and held up the envelope she'd received. "What do you know about this? Where'd it come from?"

Jay shrugged. "I have no idea. I went to check the mail and that was the only thing in there. I brought it up to slip under your door, but left it in the kitchen when I put my groceries away. It's when I got to my room that I noticed you had already picked up the mail."

Shanae sighed, "Okay, then."

Jay sensed drama, "Why, what's wrong? Is it a death threat or somethin'?" he asked, half serious.

"No, just bullshit as usual I guess," she replied fanning off his concern with a wave of her hand. "Let me let you get back to Donna."

"Okay girlie, sorry I couldn't help you."

Jay closed his door and took a deep breath as he shook his head, "That girl got man trouble again. I'm sure of it."

£

Lowell became quite the pro at navigating Facebook in the weeks following Jerry's barbeque. He'd accepted Danicka's friend request and became a friend of Melanie's as well. They communicated here and there, just generic stuff mostly however, he frequented her page perusing her many photos and posts to see what was going on in her life. He was pleased to see that she had posted several pictures of Rhianne in different stages of her growth over the years. One photo in particular threw him for a loop.

In it, Melanie was stooped down hugging Rhianne and Rhianne's back was to the camera. They must have been at the beach or pool given their attire. Rhianne's bathing suit allowed her bare back to be shown off. On her left shoulder blade, there was a small dark mole. This feature may have been insignificant to the average person, but for Lowell it was like figuring out the last piece of a complicated puzzle.

He'd reached under his t-shirt and fingered the mole on his own shoulder blade that was a perfect match to hers. At that point, he knew Rhianne was his and truth be told, he didn't want to go on another day without being able to speak that fact aloud. Come what may he had to tell Giselle that he had a ten-year-old daughter.

No time was ideal to spring that type of news on someone, but when Giselle began one of her many hypothetical circumstances of them having a child together, Lowell couldn't hold it in anymore nor did he want to.

They were lounging on the sofa in the living room enjoying some late night shows while the kids were asleep. Giselle was lying down with her head in Lowell's lap while he caressed her absentmindedly. As soon as she mentioned a baby, he tensed up and being pressed against him, Giselle took notice. She sat up on the natural hued sofa to face Lowell, her bottom lip slightly pushed out.

"What's wrong?" Lowell felt his chest tighten as though the late Michael Clarke Duncan was giving him a bone crushing squeeze. He straightened his back and adjusted himself to sit up straight at the edge of his seat. Giselle watched closely as he twiddled his thumbs, fingers interlocked, eyes on the carpet before they abruptly met with hers.

"Giselle, you know I love you more than life itself and I would never do anything to hurt you intentionally. So before you start thinking the worst I'll tell you right now I have never cheated on you, never even thought about it. You are the only woman I want and I'm gonna make you my wife, there's no doubt about that."

Giselle felt a little relief because she believed him. After all, he had never given her any reason to doubt him. It was the distressed sound of his voice and the nervous thumb twiddling that led her to believe there was cause for alarm. And then there was the fact that he didn't say, 'And I want you to have my baby.' She wanted to ask him to cut to the chase but was afraid of what the answer might be.

Before she could contemplate it, he continued, "I also want you to have my child. Thing is, there are some things I have to tell you that are definitely gonna be life-changing; for you, for me, the kids…all of us. I could have told you this when we first got together, but I just, just found out that it really is true. That what I thought all these years is actually a reality."

Giselle started to get worried all over again. Hearing Lowell's strained voice was bad enough, but listening to his tone was eerie. It was almost as though he was talking to himself and was just starting to get "it" whatever "it" was. "Low, you're scaring me," she voiced.

"Giselle…" He took her hands in his. "When I went into the service I knew there was a possibility that I had a baby on the way," he spit out. Giselle tried to pull her hands from his but his tight grip didn't allow her to. "Listen to me, please."

She bit her lip but kept her hands still.

Lowell took a deep breath before he went on, "Like I said, I knew there was a possibility but there was never any confirmation. No one ever called me, emailed, texted, or showed up on my doorstep. And I damn sure didn't get any child support summonses or anything. So although I assumed there was a baby on the way, I just put it in the back of my head and went on with life because it didn't seem like I was right. I finished up my run in the army, met you and fell in love. I'm not gonna sit here and lie and say it didn't cross my mind every now and again because it did. But when I started having all the health issues I really started thinking about my life, death…everything. And I knew that if I had a child out there child there was no way I could go on without knowing him or her."

Giselle bit the inside of her bottom lip. She couldn't explain the tears building up in her eyes, but they were there nonetheless.

"You know I have the Facebook account and got in touch with my old friend Jerry."

"Mmm hmmm."

"Well when he mentioned that my ex-girlfriend was gonna be there I figured I could pass through and just put the issue to bed. Find out if she had my child and just didn't tell me."

The grip Lowell had on her hands had loosened and she seized the opportunity to free her hands of his. She stared at Craig Ferguson on the television but Lowell had her ears at his disposal.

"So yes, I went there not only to see Jerry, but with the ulterior motive of seeing Melanie." Lowell wasn't planning to hold anything back. He was just going to put it all out there and deal with the consequences. Giselle knew of Melanie and that they had a bad break-up but that was about it. Once he explained everything in detail, he felt she would understand, but he knew it wouldn't be an easy road.

Giselle couldn't stay silent any longer. Her voice a mixture of fear and frustration she asked, "You told me you broke things off with her. Did you leave her because she got pregnant Lowell...do you have a child or not?"

"I told you, I didn't know anything for sure and that's the truth," he said looking at her pointedly. "I do know Melanie has a ten year old daughter who was there with her. Her name is Rhianne and she has a lot of my features, Gis. I didn't ask...I don't know... I just couldn't. It was a bit overwhelming to tell you the truth," he paused briefly to get his words together.

"I became her friend on Facebook so I could look though her pictures for Rhianne and just basically find out what I could before I approached her about it. That's where I saw this one of Rhianne with the same birthmark I have in the same place. Giselle, that little girl is mine."

Giselle just sat there, the tears now running silently but freely.

Lowell touched her thigh, "Say something. Please."

She wiped the tears with the back of her hand before finally speaking her thoughts. "What do you want me to say, Lowell? You drop the bomb on me that you have a ten year old daughter. Ten years old!" she said trying not to raise her voice and wake her children.

"What am I supposed to say to that? And then you tell me you left knowing that you may have had a child but you say that's not your reason for leaving. So if you didn't leave to run away from your responsibilities, then why did you leave?" Giselle's hurt and disappointment was rapidly upgrading to anger. She didn't want anything in Lowell's past to tarnish the image she had of him. She knew he cared deeply for both Marcelle and Nicola in fact, he loved kids in general. Knowing that, she couldn't wrap her mind around why he would break up with Melanie and leave knowing fatherhood was a possibility.

Lowell breathed in deeply through his nostrils. He knew she had every right to be upset and when he explained the rest of the somewhat complicated situation to her he knew things wouldn't get much better.

"Giselle, I didn't break up with her to run away from anything. I have no problem taking care of my responsibilities and that's why I'm gonna do whatever it takes to correct this situation. I'm gonna confront her and get a paternity test and if my suspicions are correct, I'll make sure I do everything in my power to be there for that child."

His words were commendable but Giselle couldn't help feeling cheated in some way. If this was true, her dream of having Lowell's first child would remain just that, a dream. She sat there and willed herself not to be selfish; there was an innocent, young life to consider after all. But something didn't sit well with her.

"Lowell you didn't answer my question. Why did you break up with Melanie?"

Lowell ran his hands over his face and leaned forward, resting his elbows on his knees, his hands clasped together.

"Giselle, I am not proud of everything I've done in the past. As a youth, I've made decisions I wish I could go back in time and change. The situation I'm about to explain fits in that category for sure."

He reached over and snatched the remote control off the coffee table to alleviate the only possible distraction in the room. With the television turned off he was sure he had her full attention; he didn't want to have to repeat what he was about to say. With Giselle's eyes curiously scanning his face, Lowell proceeded to fill in the blanks about his past with Melanie and his sudden departure.

A little over an hour later with all the facts laid out and nothing left to tell, Lowell felt a sense of peace, however short-lived. Giselle still needed time to process all that she'd been told. It sounded like a soap opera to her but she knew it had to be true. There was no way anyone could make that up.

She started out being angry with him, but knew there was no rewinding time; he couldn't ask for a do-over. Regardless, she shed many tears on the sofa that night and Lowell shed some too because how was he to know that a stupid decision made over ten years ago would have an effect on his current relationship? Lowell knew he could get through it all once Giselle expressed that she would be there for him. He still had to speak with Melanie and reveal things to her and he didn't think he could do it without Giselle's support. He knew he was blessed to have a mate as understanding and loving as her. When they finally made their way to bed that night, Lowell thought to himself, Half the battle is over, but Lord please give me the strength to fight the bigger battle that lay ahead.

Chapter 11

Timothy lay in his bed atop the multi-colored comforter with his cell phone in one hand and his erect member in the other. Displayed on the screen of his phone was a close-up headshot of Shanae, her plump mauve lips turned up into a smile, her eyes staring seductively at the camera, head cocked to the side teasingly.

Concentrating on the photo with half closed eyes, Tim proceeded to run his hand up and down his shaft applying pressure where needed to satisfy his demented sexual urge. The image on his phone was actually a picture of a picture of Shanae that adorned her work station. The minute Timothy noticed it, he knew he had to have it as part of his running collection. When the opportunity arose, he wasted no time saving the image to his phone.

Now, as he approached the brink of ecstasy, thoughts of Shanae in countless sexual positions flooded his mind. He continued to jerk, pull, and tug at his dick gaining momentum when he remembered the last time they were together and anticipating the next time he would be inside her warmth. He came hard and intense leaving traces of his cum on the comforter and the jeans he had barely pulled down.

Exhausted, he fell into a deep slumber not bothering to clean up his mess.

Penny returned home from her trip to the stores a short while later. She was satisfied with her recent purchases and hoped Timothy would appreciate the items she bought with him in mind. The apartment was quiet except for the faint sound of the bedroom television in the distance.

After a quick stop in the kitchen for a bottle of water, she entered the bedroom and was immediately repulsed at the site that greeted her. It wasn't unusual for her to find Timothy laid out and exposed after apparently pleasuring himself, but it was becoming too frequent for her taste.

She stood there for a moment, bags in hand, watching her husband sleep. Dry semen covered his exposed, shriveled penis and left white marks on their freshly washed comforter.

At the sight of his cell phone right next to him, Penny felt a knife go through her heart. She knew whatever he was doing to get his rocks off involved "Sexy Shay." She'd caught him staring at the pictures of her in his phone enough times to know Timothy was completely obsessed with this woman. Penny saw red as thoughts of this well-shaped woman sexually satisfying her husband flooded her mind.

She didn't give a shit if it was in person, via text, phone calls, photo sharing or video. All she knew was that this Shay person was taking up too much of her husband's attention and she, his wife received even less of his time than she already had. She dropped the bags where she stood and began calling his name.

"Timothy...Timothy!"

Timothy shifted into a more comfortable position and continued to nap. Penny walked over to the TV and blasted it during an Allstate Insurance commercial. She found it ironic that Timothy opened his eyes when the deep-voiced Dean Winters asked, "Are you in good hands?"

Groggy and confused Timothy rubbed his eyes and sat up in the bed.

"What the hell is wrong with you making me jump out of my sleep like that?" he asked Penny with a menacing look on his face.

Immediately, she backed down and changed her approach; Timothy had that effect on her. "Ah, sorry I just came in to see you all exposed and thought ..."

"That's your problem. No one told you to think, you don't do that too well Penny—or have you forgotten?"

Penny bit her bottom lip and stood there awkwardly.

"Where the hell were you anyway?" he asked nastily, looking her up and down with a disapproving glare.

"I was out at the stores shopping for some lingerie," Penny said fumbling with the packages at her feet.

"Lingerie? Who the fuck you need new lingerie for? Better yet, what lingerie can your fat ass fit into?"

Penny stood there unsure if she should show him her purchases. I'm not gonna allow him to break me today. Once upon a time I was a strong woman; I need to stop being so damn weak, she thought to herself. She proceeded to retrieve a red satin and lace teddy with matching thong from one of the bags and held it up so Timothy could see it.

"I figured you'd like this. I can model it for you later," she said, ignoring his degrading comment.

Timothy regarded the items with distaste. He stood up, walked over to his wife and fingered the thong she displayed. "This shit looks like a slingshot!" He took it out of her hand and stretched the fabric at the waistband. Carefully, he placed the underwear upon penny's head as though it were a sweatband.

"There you go. I think that's a good look for you," he nodded and strolled out the room laughing to himself and leaving Penny with the thong around her head looking ridiculous.

His laugh resounded mockingly in Penny's ears bringing a flood of tears to her eyes. She blinked back the moisture that threatened to soak her cheeks, and swallowed in an attempt to maintain her composure, *This Shay bitch is gonna pay for this. If she wasn't walking around like a trashy whore, Tim wouldn't be so interested in her. I don't give a fuck, a man is gonna be a man, she shouldn't be tryin' to make him lust over her. But that's ok, I'm gonna show that bitch I mean business.*

The constant emotional abuse and cheap shots at Penny's self-esteem had her steadily justifying Timothy's reckless behavior. She was so fed up with "Sexy Shay" that she was almost ready to confront her. Almost. She knew Timothy would more than likely beat her ass if he found out that she had approached his new love interest. But Penny didn't have to confront her. She had other plans.

£

"Hey what's up, Sis?" Melanie spoke into her headset as she drove Rhianne to dance practice.

"Not much just checkin' in to see what you're up to."

"I'm driving Rhianne to the Doles Center in Mt. Vernon for dance rehearsal. Her first show is coming up, are you gonna make it?" Melanie changed lanes to prepare for her upcoming exit off the Hutchinson River Parkway.

"Yeah, you know I'm not gonna miss it. Text me the info so I can put a reminder in my phone," Shanae said as she watched Quincy get dressed.

"Okay, I'll do it when I get back to the house. I have to call Aunt Lorraine and tell her, too."

"Yeah most likely she'll be driving with me, but you know she'll be there. How's RiRi liking it anyway? I haven't had a chance to talk to her about it yet."

"She was hemming and hawing at first, once she had her first practice it was a wrap. That's all she talks about. You should see her; she watches the music channels on demand and tries to mimic their moves. It's really cute to watch. I can't wait to see her perform with her troupe. She has a mentor whose a few years older than her who helps her out with her form and pace, so she's doing well."

"That's good, I'm glad she's enjoying it."

"Oh my gosh, I've been so busy I haven't even gotten to tell you. Guess who I saw at Jerry's barbecue a couple weeks ago?" Melanie's voice rose as she became excited at the memory.

"Who?" Shanae was interested to see who her usually laid back sister was getting so animated over.

Melanie opened her mouth to speak and then glimpsed Rhianne staring back at her in the rear view mirror. "Listen, let me call you back in a few…ears."

Shanae got the hint, "Okay, I'm here," she replied before ending the call.

The entire time she was on the phone, Quincy was in a corner on the opposite side of the room texting feverishly. He was so wrapped up in typing he didn't even realize he had her full attention so she decided to see who had his.

"Who're you over there texting all crazy?"

"Your friend be buggin' yo!" Quincy said shaking his head.

"Whatchu mean?"

"She wants me to go over there and I told her I'll check her later on tonight or tomorrow and she just started wildin' out. Talkin' 'bout she know I'm with some girl and how I think I'm slick but she got my number and a whole bunch of other bullshit," Quincy explained blowing the situation off.

Regardless of Quincy's nonchalant attitude, deep down Shanae knew he had some true feelings for Maxine. She saw the way he was texting her back and swore she detected mild distress in his tone when he spoke. An attitude began to brew, but she quickly caught herself. Oh well, he ain't my problem anyway. Let Maxine deal with her man.

"So you going over there?" Shanae busied herself with channel surfing to appear uninterested.

"Nah, not now anyway," Quincy informed her as her cell phone alerted her of a new text message.

Maxine: What you up to chica?

Shanae thought fast before replying.

Nothing much. Cramps kicking my ass today.

That was a believable statement because it was common for Shanae to have really bad periods. Furthermore, she'd left work at midday to go to the dentist so Maxine had no idea what she was doing. A whole seven minutes passed before a reply came through.

Maxine: Aww damn. Going on 4th ave to shop, wanted company.

"Not today Max," Shanae said under her breath.

"Huh?" Quincy looked up from his phone where he was now checking his email.

"Nothing."

Shanae: Not today. I'm hanging out with Midol today!

Maxine: Cool, feel better.

Shanae: Thanks Max.

Shanae didn't see the point in making Quincy aware of her and Maxine's contact, so she kept it to herself. After about five minutes, Quincy prepared to leave and Shanae was about to see him out when her phone created another interruption. This time it was Melanie again.

"Hey! So yeah guess who showed up at Jerry's barbecue out of the blue," she said continuing right where they left off.

Shanae was stumped, "You know I don't have a clue."

"Friggin' Lowell. Of all people, Lowell Washington," Melanie said matter-of-factly.

"Get out!" Melanie did not expect to hear that name.

"Yes! He was there, can you believe that shit?" This was the first time Melanie was able to voice her feelings on seeing her old flame. Besides Danicka, Shanae was the only other person in her life who fully understood the impact their breakup had on her. So now, she was able to be candid and share her feelings of disbelief at his sudden presence.

Shanae was just as taken aback as her sibling was, "Where the hell did he pop up from? I didn't know he kept in touch with Jerry."

Quincy looked up briefly and started paying a little more attention to her conversation when he heard the words 'he' and 'Jerry.'

"That's what I said but apparently they reconnected on Facebook."

"Damn, that's crazy. So what did he have to say?" Shanae was interested to know why Lowell popped up on the scene after so many years.

"He was cool; he apologized for the way he left and everything. You can imagine how caught off guard I was. And I'm not even gonna lie, he was looking good, for real."

146

Shanae's brain was going a mile a minute. "Listen to you. Don't let Randy hear you say that."

"Randy is good, he ain't got nothing to worry about. I am so over Lowell and all the heartbreak I endured, but it was wild seeing him though," Melanie said almost to herself.

"I'm sure. So what's he up to nowadays? He lives in New York?" Shanae needed to know why Lowell was lurking. She was protective of Melanie and did not want Lowell coming back into their lives to shake things up. Everything was going well and Shanae needed them to stay that way.

"Yeah, he said he lives in Tarrytown and is an engineer at National Airlines. I hear he lives with his woman and her kids, so he's doing his thing," Melanie explained.

"Word? That's cool. So he ain't got no little Lowell's of his own running around, huh?"

"No, not as far as I know anyway," was Melanie's reply.

Sitting on the bed patiently waiting for Shanae to complete her call, Quincy made a mental note of the name Lowell. He knew he and Shanae weren't a couple, but he didn't know how he felt about her being with other people. They had never discussed it.

The doorbell rang abruptly interrupting the sisters' conversation. Quincy looked at Shanae quizzically. She turned her lips down and shrugged her shoulders in response, "Mel, let me go see who's at this door. I'll call you back later."

"Ok then, later," Shanae tossed her phone on the bed.

"Be right back," she said to Quincy as she went to respond to the unannounced visitor. She couldn't wait to continue her conversation with Melanie; she had more questions about Lowell's unexpected appearance.

Reaching the foyer, she pulled aside the curtain and peeked through the mini blinds of the window next to the front door. She almost threw up at sight of the figure standing on her doorstep. Shanae quickly let go of the blinds and stepped back. As if on cue Maxine knocked on the door again.

Fuck, she knows I'm right here 'cause she knows there's no way I could hear that knock from my room. Shanae swallowed, took a deep breath and opened the door.

"Hey Max, wassup? I didn't know you were passin' through."

Maxine had on a screw face and allowed her eyes to canvas everything in their path. "I'm sure you didn't. I was stopping by to check on you and maybe burn this blunt I have with me but I see you already have company," she said with major attitude.

"What the hell are you talking about?" Shanae was not about to admit anything without the evidence laid out before them.

Maxine began shaking her head as she looked at her friend. She couldn't believe Shanae was trying to play her like that; Quincy's Honda SUV with its distinctive vanity plates was clearly parked across the street.

Without saying a word, she breezed past Shanae and made a mad dash for the stairs, taking them two at a time. Shanae ran up behind her. Sitting on the bed in the room, Quincy heard what sounded like a herd of horses coming up the steps, and then the door burst open and Maxine was on him throwing fist in the air and wailing.

"You motherfucker, I knew you were fuckin' around on me. You piece of shit!" Maxine made sure each blow she threw connected with a part of Quincy's body despite his maneuvering to try to protect himself from her assault.

Shanae had reached her bedroom in time to see both of them on the bed with Maxine trying her best to straddle Quincy. She knew the mayhem before her had to end, but she thought better of putting her hands on Maxine.

"Stop it Maxine, what the fuck!" Shanae yelled from the doorway. Maxine finished off Quincy with one last slap in the face before turning her attention to Shanae.

"Shanae, who the fuck do you think you're talking to? You're supposed to be my friend and you here sleeping with my man. What kind of shit is that?" she screamed at the top of her lungs. She stood there staring at Shanae, seriously expecting an answer.

Shanae parted her lips but couldn't find her voice. She wanted to look over at Quincy but trained her eyes on the carpeted floor instead. Maxine took that as a sign of disrespect and ran over to Shanae with speed that rivaled any Olympic champion.

By the time Shanae looked up, Maxine's fist was already connecting with her jawbone. Shanae knew she was in the wrong and truly did not want to fight her friend, but at the same time, she wasn't about to stand in her own home and get the crap beaten out of her either. She lifted her hands in defense and tried her best to stop the barrage of blows being brought down on her body. The two of them were on the floor, arms and legs flailing as Quincy attempted to part them.

Jay was in his room unpacking from a show he performed the previous evening when he heard all the commotion coming from Shanae's room. The sound of glass breaking and the booms and bangs of something or someone being thrown against the walls caused him to leave his quarters to investigate. He ran to the sound of the ruckus and found himself at Shanae's room door looking down at her and a white girl going to blows. There was a guy who Jay knew only as Q trying to part them. Items from the dresser top were strewn about the room and a broken perfume bottle left glass remnants about the carpeted floor.

Jay took a deep breath and found the baritone he reserved for when he had to exert his masculine authority, "Cut this mess out and stop acting like animals before I call the police."

Almost immediately, the women stopped rumbling and looked in the direction of the authoritative command. Jay even surprised himself with the base coming from his voice. Maxine's fingers were intertwined with Shanae's Yaki weave as she looked up at Jay, clearly out of breath.

Jay lit into her, "Now I don't know who you are, but I know you don't live here. You need to get off of her and get outta here before I call the cops and have you arrested for assault," he said with his hands on his hips.

Maxine held Jay's glare as she released Shanae's locks and got up off the floor. She looked around the room at the mess, at Quincy, at Shanae laid out on the floor, and got emotional. "I can't believe you did me like that Shanae," she said her voice cracking. "I can deal with Quincy's cheatin' ass, but we've been friends too long for you to play me like this. I thought we were girls."

Shanae remained on the floor not saying a word.

"You do so much fucked up shit to so many people and I still believe in you and call you a friend and this is the thanks I get?" Maxine had tears running down her face and decided against saying anything further lest those present see her completely break down. She picked up her car keys off the floor, turned to Quincy and said, "I told your lying ass I was on to you. Don't even think about coming anywhere near me. Whatever you have at my house will be dumped on this bitch's doorstep in the morning."

She then looked at Jay as she wiped her tears away. "I'm sorry, this is not how I usually get down, but she needed her ass bust right quick," she said before adding, "Being that you know her, I'm sure you can relate." And with that, she made her exit.

Quincy knew he couldn't follow Maxine out but he needed to ensure that he was still on good terms with someone, so he got up and attempted to see about Shanae still on the floor.

"You a'ight? Come here," he said holding out his hand to her.

"Man, I'm good, leave me the fuck alone," Shanae said turning away from him. Quincy kissed his teeth, grabbed his things and left without another word.

Jay felt sorry for Shanae as she sat there on her bedroom floor looking defeated. He approached her and offered her his hand, "Come on Shanae, get up off the floor."

Shanae rested her head in her hands and started sobbing uncontrollably. As much as she tried to get herself together, she couldn't stop the tears from flowing. Maxine was one hundred percent correct with her statement. All the fucked up shit she'd done to people, men she'd crept around with, lies she'd told, Maxine was by her side and on her side through all of it.

To lose Maxine would be to lose the only person she could truly call a friend, and that hurt. Shanae wanted to get up and put on a strong front, but she was too defeated and for the first time, ashamed. The hurt in Maxine's eyes was real and she felt like a heel for having put it there. Shanae felt Jay place his arms around her and she collapsed against him, allowing herself to be comforted by a caring soul, if only temporarily.

That night Jay discovered that Shanae wasn't as big and tough as she'd like people to think. Her rugged exterior was just a façade for the scared, vulnerable little girl who he saw crumble before him. He realized that of all things, she simply needed a friend to listen, support, and most of all guide her because apparently, she was a lost soul who needed to find her way.

Jay decided that he would be there for Shanae whether she wanted him to be or not. He saw the good in her even if no one else could, and he vowed to be her friend even if no one else would. As he kneeled on the floor and held her close, he concluded that he would be the friend he wish he had when he was battling with coming out to the world as a homosexual man.

£

Since Lowell revealed his secret to Giselle, he felt like a huge weight had been lifted off his shoulders. For years, he'd been walking around with the guilt of not being completely honest with his live-in love. Now he could finally breathe easy and relax knowing that everything was out in the open and she was in his corner.

In fact, she had been pressing him to suck it up and finally confront Melanie. Giselle couldn't understand what was holding him back now that everything was common knowledge. The reality of the situation was Lowell was just nervous about the outcome and how it would change his life. He knew Giselle was right and dragging the situation out would not be fair to her.

Sitting at the computer in the living room, he logged on to Facebook and went to Melanie's page. He'd communicated with her faithfully since Jerry's cookout and felt that he had built up enough if a rapport with her to set up a face-to-face meeting. He scanned her page and read her recent posts, which were nothing serious, just her usual flippancy and random musings. An inbox message would be the best way to go, thought Lowell as he typed a brief message:

Hey Mel, please give me a call when you have a moment, 555-2121. Thanks, Low.

He hit send and logged off. It was his turn to drop Nicola to dance practice, so he went to check if she was ready. As he approached her room, he heard the sounds of "Took the Night" by Chelley and knew Nicola was practicing the dance routine she choreographed to perform with the student she was mentoring. The song was on constant replay in their house so much for the last few weeks that even Marcelle was caught walking through the house chanting, "Hate, hate, hate, hate, hate. I don't care what these chicks say!" Lowell smiled to himself at the memory.

Quietly, he peeped in Nicola's doorway and watched her go. With her back to the door, she sashayed across her room, whipped her hands in the air, and rocked her head side to side as she expertly

155

displayed her skills in movement. Lowell was always amazed at how she could put a dance to even the simplest of beats. Her choreography was quite advanced for a girl her age, and both he and Giselle knew it was only a matter of time before she was either "discovered" or recruited for a major production.

Nicola continued her routine, turning around to see Lowell doing his own comical jig while he watched her. Without missing a beat she smiled and finished dancing to the last minute and a half of the song. At the final cymbal clap, she posed with one hand on her hip and one behind her head in a 'come hither' type of stance. Perspiration trickled down her hairline and her breathing was heavy, but her form was flawless. Lowell's lone clapping although enthusiastic sounded hollow in the sudden absence of the resounding music but Nicola appreciated the recognition.

"Thank you, thank you," she said as she bowed twice, mockingly.

"Do you think you've practiced enough for practice? It's almost time to leave and Marcelle wants a ride to the field on the way."

"Ha ha ha, keep joking but my little pupil and I will put the other teams to shame at the show," Nicola said dabbing her sweat with a towel. "Lowell I'm telling you, this is the perfect routine for her because she's such a little lady. With her attitude, my routine and the words of the song…it's the bomb, for real. I can't wait 'til everyone gets to see it."

Nicola was amped about the upcoming show where each of the five troop headliners has to perform an original routine they choreographed with the child they mentored for the summer. It would be the grand finale to the Dance Pointe summer dance program recital and Nicola was even more invested than usual due to being a chosen headliner for the very first time.

"Your mom and I are looking forward to it as well, but right now you better hurry up and jump in the shower. We have to leave soon if you want to be on time."

"I'll be ready in ten," Nicola said, already grabbing garments from her drawer.

Half an hour later they pulled up in front of the Dance Pointe studios where Nicola and Marcelle both exited the vehicle; Nicola offering a hurried goodbye as she disappeared into the building and Marcelle switching seats to ride shotgun. Pausing only long enough to make sure the younger boy's seatbelt was fastened, Lowell pulled off toward the field to make his next drop off.

There's a saying, time waits for no man, and that couldn't be truer for Melanie as she almost screeched to a halt in front of Dance Pointe four minutes flat after Lowell's departure and exactly eleven minutes after roll call. Rhianne sat in the back seat with her bottom lip pushed out because as young as she was, she was a stickler for punctuality. A child that hated creating waves and drawing unnecessary attention to herself; she hated being late.

"You want me to come in with you?" Melanie asked aware of Rhianne's disposition.

"No Ma, I'm ok," Rhianne replied with a mild hint of annoyance.

She looked at Melanie and caught the brief yet evident look of pain and surprise that crossed her oval-shaped face.

"I'll see you after practice, love you," Rhianne said blessing her mother with a peck on the cheek and half hug.

I'll take it, Melanie thought as she inhaled the shampoo from Rhianne's freshly combed hair.

"I love you too," she called as Rhianne speed walked through the studios entrance. She was realizing that Rhianne was getting older and more independent. Grudgingly she concluded that she would have to little by little, start giving her, her own space. I am so not ready for a teen, or tween for that matter, Melanie said to herself as she pulled off toward the shopping center to kill time before having to return to pick up her little woman.

Chapter 12

It was early Saturday morning and Maxine was out and about running errands so that she could have the rest of the day to herself. Not that she had any major plans; since the discovery of Shanae's betrayal, she'd been keeping a low profile. The anger had subsided and hurt settled in bringing with it a bout of depression. Naturally, Maxine had not contacted Shanae since the incident, but that didn't stop Shanae from borderline harassing her.

Each day she received a minimum of three voicemail messages and seven phone calls from her former friend. She ignored each one because as far as she was concerned, there wasn't anything to talk about. The situation pretty much spoke for itself – Shanae was not only a hoe, but a hoe with no boundaries. And to add make matters worse, Maxine had to see her five days a week at the office. It had only been a week, but it was becoming noticeable to co-workers that there was a problem with their friendship. The usual lunch mates were now eating separately and no one had witnessed them chat and joke around as they usually did. As far as Timothy was concerned, Shanae was on her own.

Walking down the bedding aisle in Target, Maxine felt her phone vibrate. She knew who the caller was before she even checked and sent them to voicemail without a second thought. Shanae's calls were getting earlier but the ignore feature on Maxine's phone worked all times of day. After picking up two new pillows and a mattress cover, Maxine browsed the area rugs before taking her purchases to the front of the store to check out. The store was unusually crowded for it to be only after nine o'clock in the morning but it was Saturday after all, and there were several cashiers open so the lines weren't long.

She placed her items on the belt and perused the magazine rack as she waited for her turn. Her ears perked up when she heard a familiar name and she looked over in the direction that it came from.

One register over and paying for his purchase was none other than Tremaine. He didn't notice her and Maxine was just fine with that, as he had some interesting company. A beautiful dark-skinned female with what was what appeared to be a well-made lace-front wig stood next to him ready to push the cart.

Maxine laughed inside and was glad that Shanae wasn't with her. Who knows how she would have reacted. He was laughing with his companion and Maxine wished him the best. I don't know who she is, but she's bound to treat him better than Shanae. She shook her head and greeted the pimple-faced cashier who was ready to ring up her merchandise.

HOEISM: BORNTODOIT

£

The past week had been a busy one for Melanie as she'd picked up extra hours working at a few clinics she was affiliated with. Her hectic schedule called for Randy to step in and help with dropping off and picking up Rhianne from dance. She had hardly seen either of them all week and looked forward to the date night she and Randy had planned for that evening. Rhianne would be spending the night with Aunt Lorraine who had volunteered to pick her up later that evening.

Melanie relished the time to herself and after sleeping late, showering, and eating a light breakfast of egg whites and spinach enveloped in a whole wheat wrap and fresh fruit, she opened up her iPad and logged on to Facebook. She checked her notifications, visited and posted in a few groups she was in, and then went to her inbox that indicated she had two unread messages.

The first was from her friend Alyssa and provided a new email address and cell phone number. Guess no one needs to physically call anymore when they have Facebook at their fingertips, thought Melanie as she wrote down the info. She went to the next message and was surprised to see it was from Lowell. She read the one liner and sat there puzzled.

I wonder what he wants. Melanie was okay with exchanging pleasantries and commenting on random posts via Facebook, but speaking with him on the phone was another story. She tried to surmise what he wanted and came up empty. She jotted down his number under Alyssa's info and made a mental note to call him. Perusing Facebook for a short while longer, she soon grew bored with that and logged off.

She picked up the phone and called her sister who she hadn't heard from in a few days. When she got the voice mail she left a brief message and hung up. No less than five minutes later, she received a text from Shanae.

You called. What's up?

Melanie kissed her teeth and sent back, CALL ME!

Shanae of all people knew how much she hated to call people only to receive a text in return. If she wanted a text she would have sent one in the first place, was her logic. Forty-five minutes went by before Shanae blessed her with a return call.

"Hey Sis, what's up?"

"I haven't heard from you in a few days so I was checking up on you. How're you doin'?" asked Melanie.

"Ain't shit, just life and all its BS," Shanae answered resigned.

"Well don't you sound like a ray of sunshine? What's got you down?"

"Nothing..."

"Sounds like something to me," Melanie pressed.

"Mph,"

"Ooookay, well since you don't want to tell me what's wrong with you, I'm gonna tell you why I'm buggin' right now. Friggin' Lowell sent me an inbox on Facebook asking me to call him."

"Word? What does he want?"

"I have no idea. Been trying to figure that out ever since I saw the message."

There was silence on the other end.

"Hello?"

"Yeah I'm here. Just thinking about what he could want from you after all these years," Shanae responded.

"No clue but, I'm gonna call him. Not sure when, but I will. It's just weird how he pops up after all these years and now wants to keep in touch. I told Randy about him showing up at Jerry's."

Shanae was a bit surprised. "Oh yeah, what'd he say?"

"You know Randy, it takes a lot to get him worked up. He just said at least he apologized and was a man about it. But I'm not sure what he's going to say about this request," Melanie said letting out a long breath.

"Oh, you're gonna tell him?"

"Yeah, why not?"

"Nothing, I just thought it'd be bringing unnecessary drama or whatever."

"Not telling him would be creating unnecessary drama because if he found out otherwise, I'd be suspect. I have nothing to hide and Randy and I don't keep secrets."

"I hear you, I agree," Shanae answered in a far off voice.

"You sound weird today; you ready to tell me what's wrong?"

"Nothing, I'm fine. Listen someone just rang the bell let me go."

"Liar! But it's all right I'll talk to you," Melanie allowed Shanae to dodge the issue, but she knew whatever it was would come out sooner or later. Shanae was forever needing her help.

£

Shanae lay in her bed stuck with the phone still in her hand. She couldn't stop thinking about Lowell's request for Melanie to call him. She ran numerous reasons around in her head and kept ending up at the same conclusion. That motherfucker better not be coming around to create drama. Everything was just fucking fine!

Tears gathered in her eyes and broke free, running down her cheeks and onto her pillowcase. She didn't bother to wipe them away, instead completely breaking down, sobs rocking her core. She buried her head in her pillow to muffle the sounds of her distress. Her mind played out the scene from a week ago when Maxine showed up unannounced.

She cried harder knowing that she couldn't even call her now and talk to her about her concerns with Lowell. There were no other friends for her to call and confide in. Sure she had acquaintances that she lollygagged with, but no one with whom she'd consider getting personal. Right now she needed someone to talk to, and even though Melanie was willing to lend her ear, Shanae was not going to accept it. She was truly ashamed at the mess her life was becoming and the less people who knew it, the better.

First being caught with the vacuums, and then breaking up with Tremaine, followed by the fight with Maxine, and now Lowell's mysterious appearance. She didn't know how much more she could take but she knew something had to give. The first step to getting herself together meant taking down Timothy and stopping the blackmail. This meant enacting the plan that she and Maxine had put together.

Now with the two of them at odds, she wasn't sure how it was all gonna play out. One thing was for sure, she wasn't going to nix the plan. It was genius, and the only thing they could think of to get Timothy off her back. Monday was two short days away and the day that she planned to put the plan into action. She had already received approval to work overtime next week and would be going in to work early Monday to begin entering a backlog of purchase orders. All she had to do was call Timothy and use her brain on him.

Shanae drug herself out of bed and schlepped across the hall to the bathroom. There, she washed and moisturized her face and dropped some visine in her eyes to battle the redness her tears had left. She grabbed a bottle of water from the fridge on the way back to her room and locked the door behind her. She chugged half the bottle and took a few deep breaths before grabbing the phone and slowly dialing Timothy's number. She held back the bile that rose in her throat as she pretended to be into him and interested in what he had to say. All she needed to do was entice him into going to work an hour early on Monday and everything else would take its course. Timothy answered after two rings.

"What's up Sexy?" He held his handset at his ear even though he was driving.

"Nothing but you."

""Is that right?"

"Mmm hmm, I dreamt about you last night," Shanae lied.

"Did you now?" Timothy said, moving his palm to shift his manhood.

"Yes. I'm ready for another episode."

"Oh yeah, you want to see me tonight?"

I don't want to see you any night. "I was thinking we could do one of the role plays you love. I've been feeling kinky as shit lately," she rolled her eyes to the ceiling.

Timothy grinned wide with his lips together and nodded his head. "I knew you'd get into it, always acting like you ain't down."

Fuck you. "Oh, I'm down, but I can't tonight. Plus, I wanna do something real freaky and where I wanna go we ain't got access to now."

He was intrigued, "Where you wanna go?"

"The office," Shanae said and held her breath.

"What? That's played out. We al-"

She exhaled into the receiver, "See I should have known you weren't on my level, nicca. I ain't talkin' the fuckin' supply closet or the bathroom like your boring ass is used to," she said naming places he had chosen for them to fuck before.

For a brief instance, he felt a jab at his pride, but he recovered when he remembered that Shanae was no stranger to sex. He figured she must have some real freaky shit up her sleeve that she hadn't shown him yet and she seemed really into it from what he could hear.

"A'ight, lemme hear what your nasty ass has planned," he said pulling over and placing his car in park to end his risk of getting a ticket and to give her his full attention.

Carefully, Shanae explained how everything was to go down for their next office romp. Timothy had to admit, it was a hell of a raunchy idea and he couldn't wait to act it all out. Then he realized he may have a problem when she said, "I already got clearance to work an hour and a half early on Monday to enter PO's, so I'll be in at seven."

"Damn, so what about me, it's too late for me to get approved for OT," Timothy whined.

Shanae had already thought about that. "So what, who says you have to work? All you really have to do is be in the building early. No one is gonna be there but me. Ben unlocks the doors at seven then goes back to the warehouse. He doesn't even know when the first employee arrives.

"Word, you're right. You have this all set, huh?"

"I thought it was time for me to take charge and stop leaving everything up to you. Believe it or not, I can teach you a thing or two. I've got some skills yet to be uncovered by you, ya know."

"Okay, well Monday you better bring your ass to work ready to be spread out, open wide, and uncovered then," he laughed in a perverted tone.

Shanae simply bit her tongue and dropped back against her pillows, relieved that her plan seemed to be coming together.

£

Sunday morning was bright and the birds chirped a happy song while a warm breeze filtered through Giselle and Lowell's bedroom blinds.

Giselle was still in the comfort of her bed wrapped in the sheets, and even though she was awake, her eyes were closed. She lay listening to the random noises from outside that carried through her window. From what she could tell, it was a beautiful day and folks were off to an early start.

Even Lowell had gotten up over an hour ago and was milling around the house. Still lying down, she stretched her tight limbs and finally opened her eyes. She sat on the edge of her bed, slid on her favorite slipper socks then padded to the bathroom down the hall. The strong scent of Clorox and Fabuloso hit her when she entered and she was thankful that Marcelle had gotten an early start on his weekend chores.

Freshened up and ready to see what everyone else was up to, Giselle descended the steps and entered the living room, joining the rest of her family that were surrounding the computer for some odd reason.

"Morning," Giselle greeted everyone.

"Morning," Marcelle and Lowell replied while Nicola looked up excitedly and waved her over to the PC.

"Ma, you gotta check this out. Miss Kiara took video of us practicing and posted it on You Tube. She did it last night and we have fifty-three hits already."

"Yeah Ma, it looks good and Nicola's head looks extra big in the video," Marcelle quipped then dodged a swat from his sister.

"Oh let me see." Giselle stood behind the chair and leaned over Nicola's shoulder. She watched as the girls of Dance Pointe pranced around the stage to Party Rock by LMFAO. Nicola was front and center and loving every minute of it.

Halfway through, the song switched and 'Sexy and I Know' had the girls each doing a hip hop inspired solo. When each girl stepped forward to do her part, a younger girl appeared from the wings of the stage to join her and when they were done, they strutted off the stage together.

Nicola was the final dancer on stage when a pretty young girl made her way from off the side to meet her. Together they did their quick piece and ended the performance. Giselle applauded happily and hugged her daughter around the neck.

"That was great, Nic. Are you all performing that at the finale?" she asked. As Nicola replied Giselle eyes caught Lowell and the awed look on his face. He looked like he just saw the walking dead.

"…of other songs 'cause Miss Kiara wants the real routines to be a surprise," Nicola was saying. Giselle slightly shook her head and put her hand on Nicola's back.

"Uh, yes let everyone be surprised. But that was an excellent practice run, right Low?" Giselle purposely brought him into the equation.

"Yeah, it was on point as usual. So who are the smaller girls?" Lowell tried to sound regular, but the hand in the pocket of his sweats was tapping to a nervous beat.

"You know about the little girls we're mentoring this summer. Remember? And me and Rhianne are dancing to 'Took the Night' by Chelley."

"Rhianne?" Giselle didn't skip a beat.

Nicola laughed, "Yeah, some of the girls call her Rhianna because it's almost spelled the same way. But that's my little prodigy; I told you she was a natural.

You gotta see her in action. Ya'll wanna see the other clips?"

"Right after I get some tea, Nic, Low did you drink tea yet?" Giselle looked him dead in the eyes.

"Nah, not yet," he said grabbing his stomach.

"No wonder you look like you're about to fall over. You know that's not good for your condition," Giselle scolded as she walked into the kitchen.

Lowell followed her leaving Marcelle starting up the Xbox and Nicola still at the computer.

Once in the kitchen Giselle rinsed, refilled and started the electric kettle, then turned to Lowell.

"Are you telling me with that look on your face that that is Rhianne? The Rhianne?" Giselle spoke in a hushed tone standing next to Lowell who dropped himself in a dining room chair.

"Yeah, that's her. When you look at it and the camera zooms in on her face, you'll see it. Damn, this is crazy," Lowell smiled and shook his head.

"Too much is what it is," Giselle was playing it cool, but she was eager to take another look at the video and study the little girl's face. "Did get in touch with Melanie and let her know you need to speak with her?"

Lowell stood and held onto Giselle's hands, "I told you I did. I'm still waiting for her to get back to me. She's probably trying to figure out what the hell I want."

"I'm sure," Giselle leaned into Lowell's arms. "I wish she would hurry up though."

Chapter 13

Shanae woke up extra early Monday morning and immediately started preparing for the day ahead. The previous night she had painstakingly selected her outfit, a simple cotton dress with matching low-heeled sandals, and laid it across her recliner for easy access.

Now as she viewed her frame in the full-length mirror, she nodded in to herself, satisfied that her fashion choice was not provocative, but rather demure and unassuming. That was the image she needed to capture and portray as she proceeded with her plan.

Her Toyota turned into the AMP parking lot promptly at 6:53a.m. She sat in her car, nervously anticipating the events that were to take place. When the office lights flickered on at two minutes to seven, she locked up her vehicle and entered the building. She knew that everything she did would be under scrutiny so she had to make sure that she didn't appear suspicious or nervous.

Once clocked in and logged onto her computer, Shanae started entering the slew of purchase orders that filled her inbox. She was on her sixth PO when she heard someone enter their pass code and enter the building. She continued typing and didn't look up. After a few moments, Timothy appeared in front of her at his cubicle. Shanae raised her head, and when they made eye contact, he gave her a quick nod and took a seat at his desk. He could be heard starting up his computer and being that there was no prepared work for him to do; Shanae wasn't surprised when she heard him passing the time by watching videos on YouTube. She laughed to herself knowing he was unknowingly helping her seal his fate with the company.

When her computer monitor read 7:28a.m., Shanae rose from her seat with several purchase orders in hand and walked to the copy room on the other side of the office. There, she set some documents to be copied and stapled before moving to the shredder to destroy some old paperwork.

From the wide and door less copy room she had a good view of most of the office, which included the side where she and Timothy worked. He's still in his cubicle, she noted.

The heavy duty shredder jammed and stopped abruptly, reclaiming Shanae's attention. She moved around the contraption and bent over attempting to release a compartment latch so that she could investigate the problem.

After tugging at the machine several times with no success, she went to stand up straight and felt herself being pushed forward. Her left hand reached

175

out to hold onto the shredder but before she could steady herself, her bottom half was being pulled backward and her dress was whipped above her waist in one fell swoop. She looked over her shoulder and was met with Timothy's hand mushing her face into the cold metal shredder.

"Don't look at me," His voice was intimidating and gruff. The flimsy lace thong panties Shanae chose to wear that day were ripped from her body with effortless precision and replaced by Timothy's roaming hands.

Shanae tried to kick him off but slipped, and that's when Timothy got the upper hand and rammed her forward allowing her head to connect once again with the shredder.

"Agh," Shanae was genuinely hurt and pissed. "Please stop, what are you doing?" she yelled.

Timothy responded by shoving his condom covered dick into a dry, unprepared Shanae. He pressed down on her back, completely bending her over against the shredder and sinking himself further into her warmth.

He grabbed her hair and roughly pulled as he brought his lips to her ear and whispered, "I knew you wanted this, you nasty bitch. Just like all the other ones who scream no, you really mean yes. Ain't no such thing as rape just a man takin' charge," His breath was hot and tart and bona fide tears escaped

Shanae's eyes. There was a coldness in Timothy's voice that sent chills to her core and at that moment she feared him.

Pumping mercilessly, Timothy's pace increased and when he was near, he used both hands to spread her ass cheeks and push himself into her as far as physics would allow. After his release, he slowly pulled out, and pulled his shirt out of his pants in order to cover himself. He slapped Shanae on the ass, and disappeared in the direction of the men's room.

Shanae continued to play the part of the victim and crumbled to the floor in the same spot where she was just assaulted. Tears rained down her face and she wiped them away before picking up her torn undergarment and retreating to the ladies room. There Shanae looked at her watch to find that it was 7:45 a.m. and she only had a few minutes before the accounting department would start to arrive for their eight o'clock shift. She quickly cleaned herself up the best she could and slowly walked back to her desk with the torn thong wrapped in a paper towel. She arrived at her cubicle, secured the thong in her bag and sat in her chair with her head in her hands.

Quietly, she sat that way for a minute or so and realized that there was no longer sound coming from Timothy's cubicle. Shanae had no idea where he had disappeared to because him leaving was not a part of the arrangement. She quickly shut down her computer, grabbed her bag and left the building.

Approaching the lot it became apparent that Timothy had left the premises; his car was nowhere to be seen. From the confines of her car, Shanae watched as one by one, AMP staff started reporting for work. When she noticed Jessica's new Nissan Sentra pull up, she knew she had to start putting on the performance of a lifetime. She exited her car ran up to Jessica on the walkway to the building.

"Oh, hey Shanae, you scared me," was Jessica's greeting but one look at Shanae's tear-streaked face set off alarm bells in her head and she gasped loudly, "Is everything ok?"

Shanae tried to talk, but burst out crying causing the HR professional to put her arm around her awkwardly. "Oh my goodness, let's go inside. Come to my office."

In Jessica's locked office with the blinds closed, Shanae sat in the chair opposite her desk crying softly. She had just explained how she had come in to work an hour and a half early to combat a surge in purchase orders and was sexually assaulted by Timothy Starks. Jessica sat there with her mouth slightly ajar and her eyes wide with shock.

"What!"

Shanae sniffed. "I went to the copy room and was at the shredder when it jammed. Next thing I know, I'm being shoved into the shredder and my panties are being ripped off," she said producing an endless supply of tears. Jessica pushed a box of Kleenex across her desk to Shanae and took a pen and paper from her desk drawer.

She looked Shanae in the eyes. "Shanae, I know this has been a traumatic experience for you, but this is extremely serious. You're gonna have to make a statement for the company and we also have to call the police and file a report. You do understand that, don't you?"

"Yes," Shanae nodded, accepting the paper and pen.

"Good. Do you know where Tim went or where he is now?"

"No, once he left the copy room I didn't see him again."

"Ok start writing down your version of the events that took place," Jessica said and then picked up her phone and dialed an extension. "Good morning. Well not too well at the moment, I have Shanae Alexander in here and we have a situation that requires your attention. I would classify it as life or death situation, yes. Okay, thank you," she disconnected the call and asked, "Was there anyone else here when that happened?"

"Whoever opened up the front today, but they must have stayed in the warehouse. They don't usually come back up front after they open up."

Just then there was a knock on the door and Jessica rose out of her seat to open it. In walked Annette Priestly, Vice President of AMP and second-in-command to the owner, Mr .Hoffman.

"Thanks for coming down, Annette. Ms. Alexander has informed me of a sexual assault that took place here this morning involving Timothy Starks of Customer Service," Jessica informed her.

"Sexual assault?" Annette was sure she misheard what was said.

Jessica had Shanae recount her story once again. Annette's face was a wall of stone by the time Shanae spoke her last word.

"Have you called the police yet?"

"No, not yet," Jessica replied sure it was the wrong answer.

"Why not? Well first things first, pull the camera footage immediately," she barked. Those were the words Shanae was dying to hear. Annette picked up her phone and requested the Horace, the Operations Manager to pull the video from the main office and copy room cameras. He called back moments later and when Jessica hung up the phone, she instructed Annette to join her behind her desk.

"He gave me access to the program and the correct pass codes so we can view everything from here," Jessica said typing rapidly as she spoke.

"Excellent."

"Okay Shanae what time exactly are we talking about?" Annette was the most serious Shanae had ever seen her.

"I arrived promptly at seven and he came in a short while after that."

After a few moments both Annette and Jessica were steady looking at the computer monitor. When Jessica gasped and Annette's jaw dropped, Shanae was sure they were viewing the incident. Although Timothy took it too far and she was now certain that he was a sexual deviant, she could have burst out laughing at their shocked expressions.

Annette was shaking her head sadly, "Shanae, I'm so sorry this has happened. Would you like to go to the hospital, do you need medical attention?"

"No, thank you. I'm going to see my doctor in the morning though," she said handing back the completed statement.

"Well for whatever reason, he was wearing a condom; he put it on right at his desk. I can't believe this happened," Jessica was in disbelief.

"Oh my God!" This was news to Shanae. She was sure he always used one with her, but to put it on at his desk. What an idiot, she thought but thanked him silently for his fuck up.

"Excuse my language but what the hell was he doing here at that hour anyway?" Annette questioned. "His shift begins at 8:30 a.m. every day."

"I'm calling Trish right now," Jessica said as she dialed the customer service manager's extension.

"Good morning Trish, quick question for ya, was Timothy Starks approved to come in early and work extra hours this morning? Oh, he is? No, no please don't say anything but there is a situation that occurred that he will be called in for. I will update you once we get to the bottom of it. Okay, thanks," Jessica disconnected the line and turned to Annette.

"He just arrived and Trish says she did not approve OT for him, but she did for Shanae and Millie who'll be coming in early tomorrow. Also, Mr. Starks just arrived for his shift."

Annette turned to Shanae. "Okay Shanae, we're going to have to get a statement from him also. We're calling the authorities because the videos clearly show an assault taking place. I'm gonna ask you to step into the conference room while we speak with him."

"Sure no problem," Shanae grabbed a handful of tissues for good measure and prepared to follow Annette into the secluded conference room. As soon as they cracked the door, Shanae could feel eyes on her. She was sure her co-workers were wondering why she was in human resources with the VP, All except Maxine. If she was there, she should have been able to put two and two together but Shanae refused to look up and make eye contact with anyone. She had to stay on her game.

"All right, just hang out here for a while. We'll call him in and get his statement, but in the meantime we will call the cops because regardless of what he says the video speaks volumes."

Shanae nodded meekly, "Thank you."

Annette left the conference room and went straight over to Harry, the maintenance man, and made an unusual request. "Harry, when Timothy gets up from his desk, do me a favor and collect his trash, but don't throw it away, keep it separate for me."

Harold squeezed up his face as if to say, "Huh?"

"Just take it into my office and leave it there. And leave a pair of plastic gloves as well," she elaborated.

He shrugged, "Okay."

From there Annette went straight over to Timothy. "Morning Timothy. Please come into Jessica's office for a minute." She walked off without waiting for an answer.

Jessica was to have called the police while she took Shanae to the conference room, so she didn't want to waste any time before they got there.

Timothy joined them in the office and once he took his seat, they hit play to display the footage on Jen's computer monitor which was now turned around for Timothy's viewing pleasure. He said nothing during the eight minutes of video and his face did not display the surprise and anger he battled with internally. He knew about the cameras in the office, but how they knew to check them, or what took place that morning, he had no idea.

When the video was over they gave him a chance to explain his actions, but he had no excuse. There was not one word that could have come from his lips that would justify his despicable behavior. Jessica asked him to write a statement to which he responded, "What I'm supposed to write down, that she was giving me some ass?"

"Excuse me?" Annette had no patience for the man. She saw how he looked at the women in the office and always felt creeped out by him. To be honest, the current situation didn't surprise her. She could see him doing something like that, "Are you saying she agreed to that?"

"Yeah, but you all are not gonna believe it so why bother?" Timothy shrugged.

Jessica's phone rang suddenly and she answered it to hear Horace telling her that the New Rochelle Police had arrived. She instructed him to usher them into conference room number one while she finished up with Timothy.

Once she hung up she pushed several pieces of paper across her desk. "Timothy based on the statement we received from Ms. Alexander and the video we just watched, I'm going have to relieve you of your duties effective immediately. Please read and sign the documents in front of you," she stated in a serious tone.

"What, are you fucking kidding me?" Timothy voiced. Jessica and Annette believed he was talking about being fired, but in actuality, he wanted to know what they meant about a statement from Shanae. At that point it still had not fully registered that he had been set up, but within minutes it would seep in.

Annette wanted him out of her sight so she asked, "Are you going to sign the papers?"

"No," was his short and sweet response.

"Very well, follow me," Annette said walking out of Jessica's office and into conference room number two. She asked Timothy to take a seat which he did against his better judgment. She left him alone for a minute while she went to the first conference room where Shanae had just finished giving her statement to the police. She made sure the cops had everything they needed before allowing Shanae to take the rest of the day off with pay.

She then led the cops into the second conference room where Timothy was waiting for them. While they interviewed him, she went into her office and sifted through the garbage from Timothy's cubicle. Disgusted, she bagged the condom wrapper and XXX magazine pages that she found. She was a diehard forensic science junkie and knew the find would add to any case against Timothy.

When she made it back to the conference room, they were done with Timothy and he was escorted out of the building without being allowed to clean off his desk. If he was lucky, he'd get what few items he'd left in the mail.

Annette spoke with the officers and provided them with her bagged evidence and a copy of the video. When they left, she informed Trish of the status of her two employees without divulging the private and confidential details surrounding it. Trish didn't express any regret about Timothy's departure. Annette didn't think anyone in the office would.

£

Penny wondered why Timothy's car was parked outside when she knew he should have still been at work. She entered their apartment cautiously because there was no telling what mood he would be in and she didn't have the strength to deal with one of his tirades.

She entered their kitchen she found Timothy at the dining table with a glass of brandy in front of him, the half empty bottle an arm's reach away with the cap off. Penny knew whatever was going down wasn't good; Timothy only drank when he was pissed.

"Hey, surprise seeing you here," She decided to use the light-hearted approach.

"Yeah, I thought I lived here," Timothy slurred.

"You know I mean at this hour," she said taking a seat next to him and kicking off her shoes. "How come you're not at work?"

Timothy rolled his eyes up into his head like he was really concentrating. Truthfully, he was just thinking about what to tell her to not make her upset about him losing his job. He was livid with Shanae for reporting the incident; there was no other way for HR to know what happened. She had to have planned it and for that, he wanted her to pay. It was beyond him why she refused to press charges; she took it that far, she might as well had. He'd called her a few times but she hadn't answered. He knew how easy it was to manipulate Penny and get her head all fucked up so he dropped her some bait.

"This bitch got me fired today talking about how I sexually harassed her."

"What? Who said that?" Penny was instantly interested, her eyes turning to slits.

Timothy kissed his teeth, "This stupid bitch that sits behind me. Telling HR how I came up behind her in the copy room and rubbed on her ass," he lied.

"So how did they just fire you on her word?" Penny wasn't a complete idiot.

"Fuck, I just lost my job and you wanna be askin' me all these questions. She fuckin' lied and she has more seniority than me so they got rid of me to keep her from being a pain in their ass, okay? Damn man, can I just drown my sorrows in peace?"

Penny knew better than to continue her questioning, but she had to know. "So who's the bitch that lied?"

Timothy downed the remaining liquid in his glass and looked his wife straight in the eyes. "Shanae Alexander."

£

Melanie arrived at PF Changs China Bistro twenty minutes early. She got a table and ordered an extra strong pina-colada while she waited for the other half of her party to arrive.

Her early arrival was not by accident, she had to calm her nerves. Her agreement to this meeting was not out of desire, but more out of curiosity than anything. She needed to know what was so important that a face-to-face meeting was required. Lowell wouldn't offer any details, only that it was serious. Randy encouraged her to go and didn't see why she would be feeling some kind of way about the request. But then, he was a man and must have thought it was okay to leave someone without reason and apologize ten years later. Yet still, she agreed that she should at least hear what he had to say.

There she sat in a secluded booth of the Chinese restaurant awaiting her former teenage lover when he appeared before her without notice.

"Hey there, how are you?" Lowell asked as he leaned in and planted a peck on Melanie's cheek.

"I'm great, thanks. It's good to see you again," She smiled politely.

"Same here."

Their waiter emerged, introduced himself, and began mixing sauces before them. He recited the day's specials, took their orders, and disappeared into the kitchen.

The couple engaged in trivial conversation while they waited on their meals. Lowell's rum and coke was delivered and then shortly after that, their piping hot dishes were presented. Left alone to partake of the meals, they wasted no time putting forks to mouths. They still chatted while they ate and

Lowell strategically maneuvered the conversation around to kids in general and then to Rhianne.

Melanie informed him that she had recently taken up dance and was excited about it. He took that as his cue to get into the reason for their meeting. His Mongolian beef was almost done and he pushed his plate forward and looked at Melanie.

"Funny you should mention that because I found out some coincidental news this past weekend. My soon-to-be step-daughter attends Dance Pointe Studios," he kept his eyes on her as he spoke.

"Really? Small world, what's her name? Not that I know the students, but I can ask Rhianne." She was awed by the fact.

"Nicola McGreggor."

"No, you've got to be kidding. She's Rhianne's mentor," Melanie's voice rose with excitement.

Lowell smiled and nodded. "Yeah, I found that out when I saw her on the You Tube video. I was like, 'is that who I think it is,' so when Nicola said her name, it was a wrap."

"Wow, that's crazy," Melanie said before eating the last of her lettuce wrap. "But I know you didn't bring me here to tell me that."

Lowell shifted in his seat. "No, I didn't. Look I've thought about this moment ever since I saw you at Jerry's and there is no way at all to make what I have to say easy. I ask only that you hear me out fully because this is a lot."

Melanie was nervous but wanted to know what was going on. "Okay."

She watched him wipe his eyes and take a deep breath before opening his mouth and flooring her with a barrage of words that she wished she had never heard. Even though she wanted to interrupt, she couldn't. She couldn't pull air into her windpipe to produce a sound. When he was done, he just stared at her as if he wanted to cry, but it was her eyes that produced tears.

They both sat there for almost a full minute before Lowell spoke. "Say something...please."

Melanie swallowed the lump in her throat and took an audible breath before she was able to speak. "I'm gonna need you to repeat that," her words came out sounding a little more serious than she intended; her emotions were taking over.

Lowell ran a hand over his head and dropped it in his lap before honoring her request. "The reason I didn't continue our relationship when I joined the service was because I had slept with your sister. When you told me she was pregnant and didn't know who the dad was I hauled ass out of fear. I'm not proud of that and I know now that it was immature. For years I was unsure if she even had the baby, but when I came home I heard talk that she did. Word on the street was that she gave you custody and you were raising the child as your own. I battled with just leaving it alone for a long time, but when I was diagnosed with Type 2 Diabetes I knew I didn't want to have a child out there at risk not only for that, but any other health issues that may not be detected yet. The last thing I wanted to do was disrupt your life, but I just have to know."

While Lowell talked, Melanie studied his features and compared them to Rhianne's. By the time he was done, she had butterflies in her stomach. Silent tears rolled down her cheeks and she made no effort to wipe them away. If what he was saying was true, she was raising her high school sweetheart's daughter. The same man who tore her heart out with no regard and didn't even give her a do I have reason why.

"So you not only cheated on me with my sister and dumped me, but you shot your seed in her and got her pregnant, too. And here I am the schmuck who's raising the child!" her voice rising. "And what do you want anyway? I'm telling you right now you are not taking her from me. How are you even sure she's yours? Why should I believe you?" she asked although she knew in her heart it was true. Why would he go to such great lengths to bullshit her?

Lowell saw the panic on her face when she said he's not taking her and he had to nip that in the bud immediately. "Melanie I have no intention of taking her away from you. And no I don't have a paternity test to prove the fact, but when I saw her at Jerry's, it was like looking at myself. I noticed the birthmark on her shoulder and I have the exact same one. I'm sorry Melanie, but I need to know if she's mine and I want a paternity test because I refuse to be a deadbeat dad."

Melanie finally wiped her tears with a napkin when she noticed the waiter approaching. He asked if they needed anything more and left the bill, which Lowell promptly paid for with his Amex.

With their meal complete and paid for, there was no reason for them to hang around. They abandoned their booth and walked out to the garage where Melanie stopped suddenly and looked at Lowell.

"Do you know how many people this will affect? You there talking about not wanting to be a deadbeat dad, but she has a father. You can't just come on the scene and try to change our lives. You don't even know if she's yours. My sister fucked so many boys back then, shit she's still displaying signs of hoeism, so how are you even sure?" she was borderline hysterical.

Lowell wanted to reach out and hold her, but he knew better. "Melanie, I know this isn't easy, but I don't know what else to do. All I ask is that you allow Rhianne to undergo paternity testing so that we can have some closure. I'm not trying to take your husband's place and I would never undermine you. But if she is my child I want the opportunity to develop a relationship with her at the very least. I am so sorry for everything. I had no right to sleep with Shanae…"

"Damn right you didn't, she was fifteen years old to your nineteen. What the fuck!" Melanie was screaming and her voice echoed throughout the garage bringing them the attention of a few occupants. "Look I have to go," Melanie said as she practically ran across the garage to the safety of her car.

Lowell watched her leave. Although he felt bad, he knew he did the right thing. The ball was in her court now, and he prayed she thought about the situation rationally because at the end of the day, it was all about Rhianne and her well-being.

£

Hunger pangs rocked Shanae's stomach and as much as she tried to get into the episode of Dexter that she had TiVo'd Sunday night, the lack of food in her system didn't allow for it.

Giving in to her body's call for nourishment, she shut off the TV, threw on some sweats, and stepped outside. Undecided if she should grab some Jamaican food or the go-to burger and fries, she slowly walked toward the corner where she had parked upon arriving from work earlier that day.

Preoccupied with various thoughts, Shanae didn't notice the vile sight ready greet her as she approached her car. She was right upon the vehicle and prepared to insert her key into the lock when the most disgusting image cleared the fog from her mind. A piercing scream assaulted her eardrums and it took a few seconds for it to register that the sound was coming from her own mouth.

Clutching her chest, she jumped back, her eyes wide, surveying the area. Duct taped to her driver's side door was a dead sewer rat. A now bloody screw was bore through its head and imbedded into the car door lock. The rat's long tail hung from its body, flush against the car's door. The dried blood, lifeless eyes, and grey fur were an instant trigger to the bile that rose in Shanae's throat. She bent over and brought up the little contents her stomach contained.

When there was nothing left to come up, she stood straight and tried to steady herself from the sudden light-headed feeling. Quickly, she backed away and looked around for someone to help her. A few passersby glanced at her, but no one seemed interested in her dilemma. She turned on her heels and raced back to the house, and flew up the stairs to bang on Jay's door.

"What the hell flew into you today baby girl?" he said when he saw her looking somewhat wild and crazy.

Gasping for breath after her sudden sprint, Shanae held her chest and replied with a shaky voice, "Jay, someone nailed a rat to my car!"

"What?"

"You heard me someone taped a rat to my car," she said teary-eyed. The shit is gross, I can't take it off. My fuckin' stomach turned at the sight of it. Please Jay, I need you to help me out, I'm afraid of them things."

"And do what? I do a lot of things, but I don't do rats...it's just not diva-like!" Jay informed her shaking his head to get his point across.

Shanae contemplated the no-nonsense look on his face and lost it. She broke down in front of her housemate for the second time in a matter of weeks.

Totally caught off-guard, Jay wasn't sure where all this emotion was coming from. He knew she said she was afraid of rats, but this was a bit much. She was on the floor bawling with her face in her hands, sniffling and blubbering words he couldn't quite make out. He knew there had to be something more to her sudden breakdown than a dead rat and decided to do her a solid.

"Okay, okay, come on stop that and get up," he said helping her to her feet. He led her to her room and let her know he would handle the problem. "I don't know what's wrong with you lately, but whatever it is, you need to get a handle on it. I'm telling you this as a friend; you can take it or leave it. Something's there, I'm not sure what it is and it's none of my business, but you need to take care of yourself."

Shanae climbed into her bed and pulled the covers up to her chest. She nodded to let Jay know she heard him before he went downstairs to investigate. When he returned twenty minutes later he suggested she file a police report. She balked and he kindly let her know she had no choice in the matter they had already been called.

"Look, you received a letter the other day and you don't know who dropped it off, and now you have a sewer rat impaled on your car. Those things are not normal, chile. Now I'm not tryna get in ya business, I just want you to be aware and safe. I took pictures on my phone to show the cops. I'll handle as much of it as I can, but I'm sure they'll want to ask you some questions, so be ready."

Shanae was thankful for Jay's help and told him as much.

"No thanks necessary, just remember what I told you," he replied before leaving.

By the time the cops arrived and had taken her statement, Shanae was too worn out to pick up something to eat, so she ordered Chinese to be delivered. As she lay on her bed, she recounted her conversation with the officers.

When they asked her if she had any enemies or any idea who could have done that to her car, she immediately thought of Timothy. He had been calling her incessantly ever since the incident at AMP and she'd been ignoring his calls until last night. That's when she got fed up and let him have it, calling him every name in the book and let him know that he was not smarter than her even though she allowed him to think he was. She burst his bubble when she told him that he'd fed into her scheme just like she knew he would and that he could rot in hell for all she cared. The last thing she heard as she disconnected the call in his ear was him screaming that he was going to make her pay no matter how long it took.

There was a possibility that Timothy was the culprit, and the cops suggested as much when she informed them of the statement she'd made against him. She brushed it off, telling them that as far as she knew he didn't know where she lived. Furthermore, she had refused to press charges against him and when she reminded them, they pressed her to find out if he'd been threatening her. She assured the he wasn't. Now, the more she thought about it, it could have even been Maxine. She knew where Shanae lived and was still upset with her enough not to take her calls. Naw, she wouldn't do that to me. As long as I've known her, she'd never done anything so grimey. She was always the one telling me to let shit go. The one to calm me down, never the other way around. Without thinking, Shanae picked up the phone and dialed her number. To her surprise, Maxine picked up on the first ring.

"Hello."

Maxine looked at her smart phone and could have tossed it across the room that very second. She was playing Angry Birds when Shanae's call came through and her touch screen flipped over to display the caller as she was tapping, unexpectedly connecting her to her nemesis.

"Hello?" Shanae repeated.

"Yeah?"

"Hi."

"I heard you, what can I help you with Shanae? I don't have a man for you to fuck right now!" Maxine was annoyed at her casualness.

Shanae knew she had to come correct, she wasn't even expecting her to pick up.

"Maxine, I know I've said it already in the many messages I've left for you but I am sorry for what I did. I'm not expecting you to forget what happened, but I'd like you to give me another chance."

"And I'd like you to get a life. I'm not giving you another opportunity to cross me." Her tone was sharp and direct.

Shanae wasn't used to being on the receiving end of her attitude. "Max, can you at least consider my apology? I'll respect whatever decision you make, even if you never choose to deal with me again. I'd just like you to at least consider that. I've had weeks to go over the mistakes I've made and pinpoint all the chances I had to do the right thing. You were a good friend to me, without a doubt. Regardless of anything, I want you to know that I strive to be the type of friend that you've been to me. And if you do give me the opportunity, I'll show you that I'm capable."

Maxine was quiet for a moment before sighing into the phone, "I gotta go Shanae." With that, she pressed the end button, leaving Shanae to wonder if their friendship could be rekindled.

Chapter 14

"You will get through this Melanie, you have to have faith. God will see you through." Aunt Lorraine spoke softly, stoking Melanie's arm as she lay with her head in her lap.

Two days had passed since Lowell's confession and Melanie still couldn't wrap her mind around the deceit. Two people she cared deeply for had gotten together and betrayed her, and to add insult to injury, they procreated and gave her the child to raise. As far as she was concerned, it didn't get any worse than that. She hadn't yet brought herself to confront her sister.

Over the years Melanie had bailed Shanae out of countless situations, given her money, gotten her jobs, co-signed for her, and she couldn't count one single time Shanae was there for her. When fifteen-year-old Shanae came up pregnant, Melanie and her mother knew they would have a major part in taking care of the baby. Shanae was promiscuous and irresponsible from a young age and it was a given she would not be able to properly raise a child.

When their mother died, at twenty-three years old Melanie took on the responsibility of raising her niece, who to this day only knew her as mom. She knew Randy wasn't her dad, but he was her father figure and they had a good relationship for what it was worth. As unflappable as he was, Randy was rather concerned to hear what went down. Even still, he assured Melanie that it would all work out, and stressed that she should not allow their teenage mistakes to dictate who they are today.

Melanie's mind had been unsettled since she'd left Lowell at PF Changs, but she knew she could not go another day without confronting her sister.

"Auntie, what did you tell her?"

"I told her to get her butt over here as soon as possible for a family meeting. She should be here soon."

No sooner than she had spoken the words, Aunt Lorraine heard Shanae at the door. When she walked into the living room, she could tell right away that something was wrong. Melanie's eyes were red and puffy as though she'd been crying, and Aunt Lorraine's face was solemn.

"What happened, I got over here as soon as I could?" she said resting her bag on the side of the couch and took a seat.

Melanie looked at her aunt who gave her a slight nod before going right into it. "Shanae, I'm going to ask you a question that concerns the lives of several people, specifically Rhianne's, mine, and Randy's and it is imperative that you give me an honest answer."

Shanae's heart sunk the very minute Rhianne's name was mentioned. The way Melanie looked at her and spoke, she knew her decade-long secret was revealed. And while she stood there, she realized that Melanie had never said anything else about Lowell wanting to see her. With all the hoopla concerning Timothy and the odd things that were happening, she totally forgot about his sudden resurfacing. Now, looking at her sister's distressed face, she knew she had to come clean.

"Lowell," escaped her lips.

"I can't believe you would do that to me…I can't fuckin' believe it," Melanie said in a hollow tone. "Yes, you were young, but did you expect to keep this secret forever? Why didn't I deserve to know the truth?" Anger claimed her tone but she willed herself not to get up from her seat because she felt like beating Shanae down.

Shanae looked past Melanie and didn't offer a response.

"Fine, stand there and don't say anything. I have no problem doing all the talking. You fucked up big time Shanae, I mean forget about me, what about Rhianne? How are we supposed to deal with the fact that Lowell wants paternity test and to develop a relationship with her? Do you know what this all means? DO YOU?" She was screaming now, and her aunt moved closer to her just in case she made a sudden move.

Shanae knew her silence was pissing her off, but she didn't know what to say. Melanie was one hundred percent right.

"For Rhianne to know Lowell is her father means we have to tell her that you are her mother," Melanie spat. "I refuse to continue your string of lies. It's time you grow the fuck up and stop being so damn careless," Melanie was giving it to her straight. She refused to coddle Shanae for another minute. In her heart she felt as though she supported almost encouraged Shanae's bad behavior. It would come to an end right then and there.

"You better thank your brother-in-law and your aunt for me not whooping your ass. I've had two days to marinate the information. If I'd have seen you any sooner I don't know what I would've done."

There was a moment of which Aunt Lorraine took advantage.

"Shanae, that child is gonna need some form of counseling or therapy if only for a little while. This is gonna be a lot for her to process. It would have been bad enough for her to meet her dad a decade, but to find out her aunt is her mother is gonna confuse the hell out of her."

Shanae knew she had to acknowledge her aunt. "I know," she said softly.

"Auntie and I already looked into the paternity testing and once I speak with Lowell and see about his schedule, I'll make an appointment. Most likely you, Rhianne and Lowell are gonna have to do the counseling, but we'll wait and see how Rhianne handles it first," Melanie explained, all business. She was ready to move forward and not let this disrupt their lives.

"Yeah, I understand. I may need one-on-one counseling myself," Shanae said seriously. Her aunt looked at her to elaborate. "Auntie, everything Melanie said is true and lately I've just been feeling like I'm just making it. I feel like a lost soul... something's missing and I know I've been going down the wrong path, all signs say so. I haven't been living right or doing right by anyone, even myself. I thought about it the other day and as much men as I've been with, I can't honestly say that I've ever been on a date; It's always been about sex. And as selfish as I've been...I can't even say that I'm happy," she was crying now.

Melanie was shocked to hear her sister's words, but she wasn't about to appease her. She was in need of some serious tough love.

For the next two hours Shanae, Melanie, and their Aunt Lorraine talked cried and comforted each other. They were going to handle their current issue as a family as they knew they were stronger with each other's support.

Chapter 15

Maxine was en route to Mt. Vernon and hoped she didn't run into Shanae. She had recently began selling Avon for a few extra dollars and had to drop some product off to a customer. It was unusual for her do drop offs but the laundry mat attendant was recovering from surgery, and she had agreed to make the delivery.

Had she known the lady lived not only on the same street as Shanae, but on the same block, she would have declined. Because she was familiar with the area, it didn't take her long to find the house. She double parked and jogged into the building with the bag of cosmetics in hand. Five minutes later, she was back in her car about to pull off and head home when Shanae ran across her mind. Ever since she hung up the phone on her, she'd been thinking about their friendship. She always knew Shanae had issues and wasn't the most gracious person, but she was disappointed to be on the receiving end of her callousness.

Maxine actually felt sorry for her and knew she was probably her only friend. After spending so much time with her, she surmised that her behavior was actually a cry for help and there was something in

Shanae's voice the last time they spoke that led her to believe that she was truly remorseful.

Dusk settled in and the street lights were just turning on. As Maxine passed Shanae's house, she looked up at her window and saw that the blinds were closed. Approaching the end of the block, she saw Shanae's car and a figure walking around it. Shit, I hope she don't see me, she thought.

Upon closer inspection she found the person was too heavy to be Shanae, and the hair was cut low while Shanae always wore a long weave in hers. Maxine reached the stop sign and was now in line with the car. She looked over again, but the person had disappeared. Making the right turn, she looked through her rear view mirror and saw the person stooping down fumbling with Shanae's gas tank. Now that she was closer, Maxine was able to make out the person's face. Her jaw dropped when her brain registered who the lady was.

Thinking quickly, Maxine pulled over and took out her phone. She pulled up her camera and began snapping shots of the person; using her zoom feature to be sure she caught much as she could.

After snapping several shots, Maxine dialed 911 and reported an attempted arson in progress. She heard the dispatcher radio for assistance and was told to hang tight as there were several police in the area leaving an officer's funeral. Maxine hung up and saw the woman quickly walking away. She couldn't let her leave so she ran toward her calling her name. "Penny, Penny."

The woman's stride became wider and faster and although she didn't turn around, Maxine knew that it was Timothy's wife. Maxine remembered her face from the company events she'd attended over the years. Although they never spoke, just based on her actions and the way she looked at people, Maxine always got the feeling that Penny thought everyone was after her husband. Then it clicked; Shanae had been fuckin' Timothy and then ultimately got him fired. Penny was out for revenge.

"Hey Penny, I know that's you, can you come here for a minute," she yelled down the street.

Penny continued to ignore her. A police cruiser came down the block and Maxine flagged it down and quickly explained the situation to the officer who told her to go back to Shanae's car while he went around the block to detain Penny.

Maxine was standing in front of Shanae's car trying to get her on the phone when the officer returned with Penny in tow. Immediately, Penny began denying any wrongdoing, saying she was just visiting a friend. Maxine had gotten a hold of Shanae who was in her house and now on her way to the scene.

While the officer questioned Penny, Maxine took a closer at the car and noticed it had been badly keyed. She took out her phone and showed the officer the photos she'd taken just as Shanae arrived.

Presented with the hard evidence, Penny continued to deny her role in the vandalism. The officer clearly saw Penny had defiled the car and proceeded to arrest her on the spot while Maxine filled Shanae in. With Penny in the back of the police cruiser, Officer Ligorio, as his badge stated, took a statement from both women.

Shanae also mentioned the other incidents that had happened in recent weeks and suggested that maybe Penny was responsible for those as well. When the officer asked how they knew Penny, Shanae's response was, "Her husband used to work at my job until he was fired for sexually assaulting me." Before the officer could respond, Penny's jealous rage boiled over.

"Fuck you, you sloar! Ain't nobody do shit to you. You've always wanted my man. Sending him pictures of your nasty ass. Don't nobody want you!" She said hatefully through the cracked cruiser window. "You need to leave my husband alone or it's gonna be worse next time," she continued.

Officer Ligorio looked at Maxine and Shanae. "Okay, then I guess the next question would be would you like to file charges Ms. Alexander?"

"Yes."

"You can follow me down to the station then," he said walking to the driver's side of his car.

"Here Shanae, get in my car, I'll take you," Maxine said.

Shanae was thankful for the offer, and even more thankful that she was there to witness the incident.

At the station, Shanae kept her word and pressed charges, which resulted in Penny being booked for vandalism. They were unable to prove the harassment for lack of evidence, but it was obvious to Shanae and Maxine that she was the offender.

On the way home the two friends talked with Maxine, making it clear that in no way was she ready to forgive Shanae.

"I'll get there one day, but today is not that day," she had said.

Shanae was happy with that; Maxine's actions concerning the Penny incident spoke volumes to her. Maxine brought up Timothy and his departure from AMP. They joked about his downfall and how it was well-deserved. By the time they reached Shanae's house, they were in a good place. They had a long way to go before they would call each other girls again, if ever, but at least they were in the process of putting their past dilemma behind them.

£

Once Melanie had the pow wow at Aunt Lorraine's house with Rhianne, she didn't see the point in waiting any longer to seek paternity testing. Much to Lowell's relief, she called him up and together they decided on a facility and a date that they would do their half of the testing.

Lowell went the very next week and at his request, Giselle was by his side. Melanie told Rhianne she had to take a quick test at a new doctor and they went the morning after Lowell.

The three days it took for the results to come in were the three longest days of Lowell's life. When he received the results, he wept even though he already knew. He and Giselle would have to tell Marcelle and Nicola that Lowell and Rhianne were related and how. But it had to be done in time with Melanie informing Rhianne. They decided to do it the following Thursday evening, before the girls saw each other Friday night at practice.

Melanie suggested, depending on how Rhianne took the news, Lowell should pass by her house to meet Randy and more importantly, get acquainted with his daughter. She had no intention of hindering their relationship.

When Melanie received the results she had no thoughts other than how this would affect Rhianne.

She and Randy had discussed several ways to inform her who her biological parents were, but it always came back to being direct and truthful.

Thursday evening had arrived and it was time to sit her down and break the news. Melanie was a nervous wreck, but she had her husband there for moral support so that settled her fears somewhat. After Rhianne had her snack and did her homework, Melanie and Randy sat her down in the living room, telling her they had to talk about something important.

"Am I in trouble?" Rhianne asked in a cute, 'okay, what did I do now' voice.

Randy took that one, "Not at all, your mom and I just have to tell you something."

Once they were all seated, Rhianne and Melanie on the love seat and Randy right across from them in the recliner, Melanie took Rhianne's hand.

"RiRi, first thing, before anything else I want you to know that no matter what I love you and I always will. I'll always be there for you no matter what. Always remember that. You are a beautiful, smart little girl and I am so proud of you."

Randy chimed in, "Rhianne I may not be your dad, but you are my step-daughter and as far as I'm concerned you are my daughter because you make me feel like a father. I'll always be here when you need me and when you don't, I'll be there just in case."

Rhianne looked at them both slightly confused. Melanie continued before the questions began.

"Rhianne, this is probably the hardest thing I'll ever have to tell you, but you deserve to know the truth. Remember when you used to ask about your dad and I told you that sometimes adults are not responsible and don't always do the right thing?"

"Yes."

"Well, sometimes adults are irresponsible but do try to do the right thing. This may be difficult for you to understand, but as advanced for your age as you are, I think you'll get it," Melanie said then decided to stop babbling before she confused her even more. She might as well just spit it out. "Rhianne, I'm not your biological mother."

Rhianne scrunched up her face a bit and looked at Randy.

"What that means is that I didn't carry you in my belly and I didn't give birth to you. And that's all that means. Your real mother, your birth mother, was very young when she had you and she wanted the best for you but knew that she wouldn't be able to properly provide and give you all the great things you deserved. Since I was a little older, I offered to raise you as my own and because she always wanted what was best for you, of course she said yes."

Melanie held her breath knowing it could go either way from there.

A frown took over Rhianne's little face, "You mean I'm adopted?" Her tone was of disbelief.

"Yes, I legally adopted you so that you could have a good life and the opportunity to do all that you want. If your mom would have kept you, it would have been very difficult for her to give you the things you need and want. So as much as it hurt her, she allowed me to adopt you because she loved you that much."

As she took her time processing all that she was told, Rhianne wanted to make sure she understood. "So my mom couldn't take care of me, and my dad didn't want me?"

Randy had to fix that train of thought right away. "No not at all. Let your mom finish explaining it all."

Rhianne was proving she was a thinker as usual when she said, "You said you asked my mom if you could raise me. So you know her?"

"Yes, and so do you."

"I do?"

"Your biological mother, the woman who gave birth to you is who you know as your Aunt Shanae," Melanie said, watching Rhianne's expression closely.

Rhianne's mouth formed a perfect "O" before saying, "Huh?"

Randy decided to take that one. "Your mom is four years older than your aunt and when this happened they both decided that instead of letting you be adopted by a stranger, they would make sure that you were always close and that you would always know who your family was."

Melanie chimed in. "My mom, your grandmother, before she died, she had you all the time. She took care of you while I went to college. So you always had family around you. I know this is a lot of information at once, but do you understand what we're saying?"

"I think so. You and Aunt Shanae are sisters like I always knew you were, but she's really my birth mom."

"Exactly."

Rhianne sat there quietly. Melanie looked at Randy who was rubbing his beard waiting for a reaction.

"So how do you feel about that?" Randy pressed. "Nothing is gonna change as far as where you live or what you call anyone, it was just time for you to know."

"I don't know. That's cool I guess because then I really have two moms."

"Technically yes," Melanie continued to be amazed by her smarts.

"But there's a second part to the story that is a little interesting. Remember a long time ago how I said your dad was irresponsible and wasn't ready for a child something like how your mom was? Well that was a long time ago. Since then, he went to the army for a while and when he came back he was looking for you. And he finally got in touch with me," she paused to see if Rhianne had any comment about that.

"You saw my dad?" Rhianne asked.

"Yes. But I need to know how you feel about meeting him."

"Does he want to see me?"

"Very much. He knows you already have Randy and he's not looking to replace him, but he feels terrible about not being there for you. He can explain his side of everything to you in time, but he wanted you to know he wants to get to know you if you let him."

Rhianne snuck a peek at Randy who shook his head. "Don't look at me, I'm not going anywhere. You'll have two dads and two moms. That's way more than most people."

"You're not gonna be mad with me if I see him?" she asked scanning his face.

Randy cocked his head to the side, "What did I tell you earlier? I'll be here whether you like it or not. I love you and so does your mom, Shanae and your dad."

"What's his name?"

"Lowell," Melanie said waiting to see of Rhianne remembered his name.

'Lowell?"

"Yeah, does that sound familiar?"

"Kind of."

"Well how would you like to meet him tonight?" Melanie proposed.

"Really?" she said, getting excited.

"Yeah, he could tell you about himself and you two can get to know each other. I'll tell you this, he has a step-son and a step-daughter," Melanie knew Rhianne would love that fact. She was always asking why she didn't have a sibling.

"Wow! Okay, are you gonna take me to see him?"

Melanie laughed, "No, but I can ask him to come over here if you want."

"Yes."

"One more thing though. I think you already know his step-daughter. She's Nicola, your mentor at Dance Pointe."

"She's my sister? What? Nicola is my sister?" Rhianne was about to break out into a dance she was so excited.

"Something like that," Melanie smiled. "When you meet Lowell he'll explain everything to you."

"What time is he coming over?"

"As soon as I call him. But I want to make sure you're ok."

"So do I have to call him Dad?"

Randy shook his head, "No, like your mom said, nothing is gonna change but the fact that you have a bigger family."

"Okay."

"Oh, and your Aunt Shay is coming over tomorrow night to speak with you too. She loves you and she doesn't want you to be mad with her. Everything that was done was done because we all love you," Melanie reminded her.

Rhianne beamed, "I love you all, too."

Melanie gave her a tight hug. Randy joined in and they stayed like that for a few moments before separating. Melanie went to call Lowell, Shanae and Aunt Lorraine to let them know how it went while Rhianne went to prepare for Lowell's visit. Randy was happy to have that over and done with because Melanie's anticipation was driving him to drink. So he grabbed a beer out the fridge and took residence on the sofa to enjoy the rest of his rare day off.

£

"All right, so I'll be back in a couple of hours," Lowell said to his family. He had received Melanie s call an hour prior and told everyone he was going to see Rhianne.

Giselle was nervous for him because although he had already met her, she didn't know their relationship and she could have a totally different take on him. Yet and still, Lowell was on cloud nine. Nicola was just as happy because she had already bonded with Rhianne and loved her whereas Marcelle was saying he hoped Patrick and Suzy had a boy so he wouldn't be outnumbered.

"Low, tell her I said hi," Nicola instructed.

"Will do," he smiled.

He hugged and kissed Giselle on his way out the door.

"Good luck," she said as he walked to his car.

Lowell pulled into Melanie's driveway and was impressed with the size of her home. It was quite large compared to his and Giselle's. He noticed she even had a swimming pool as well. Nice, he thought to himself.

Melanie must have been looking out the window because she was already at the door when he turned up the walkway. She welcomed him into her home and introduced him to Randy who was now watching ESPN. The three of them chatted for a few minutes until Melanie called for Rhianne to come downstairs. Melanie had to smile as she appeared at the top of the steps. Rhianne had changed into one of her favorite outfits; a purple and white halter top with matching leggings. She was excited and happy and Melanie was happy for her. When she came down, Melanie introduced them.

"Rhianne, this is Lowell. Lowell, this is Rhianne."

Lowell looked at her and smiled, "Hi, Rhianne. Do you remember me?"

"Yeah, you were at the barbecue."

"Yup, sure was."

"Listen, why don't you two go into the den and get familiar with each other? I'm sure you have a lot to talk about," Melanie said leading the way.

Lowell and Rhianne sat side by side on the sofa and Lowell handed her a small stuffed bear he had bought for her. Their conversation started off a bit strained at first, each not knowing how to approach the other.

He decided to use Nicola as a common denominator to get Rhianne to open up. It worked. Rhianne was obviously very fond of Nicola and they had already bonded.

They sat in the den laughing, talking and even playing few games on the Xbox for two full hours. When he left, Lowell made sure to make a date for when they could see each other again. When he arrived home and filled Giselle in, she was happy that it went smoothly. She couldn't wait to meet Rhianne so she could welcome her into the family.

Chapter 16

Shanae was on her way back from putting a down payment on her new apartment. She had finally saved enough money to get out of the cramped room she'd been living in. There was a bit of sadness because she'd miss her housemates, especially Jay. But she knew they would stay in touch because they had bonded during Shanae's trials.

Her new part-time job as a teen mentor at the Mt. Vernon YMCA was a big factor in her increased finances. In addition to padding her pocket, it allowed her to be around young people, help them find employment, and counsel them when necessary. She came across so many young girls who reminded her of herself and she was glad she could speak from example.

Her once a week counseling sessions were also a factor in her lifestyle changes. Her counselor, Mrs. Watson, was a godsend. She helped Shanae identify her self-destructive behavior and never passed judgment. Shanae knew going to counseling was one of the best decisions she'd ever made. Another great thing in Shanae's life was that her relationships were improving. She and Rhianne were as tight as ever although it was very awkward the first few times they saw each other since the Mom news.

Maxine and Shanae's relationship still wasn't where it used to be, but they were cool and got together every once in a while. Shanae really wasn't sure if Maxine would ever fully get over the betrayal, but she was thankful to at least be given a chance.

Lowell and Rhianne's relationship was growing stronger every day and he couldn't believe that it had only been five weeks since they'd told her the news. She visited him every Sunday, and he went over to her house at least once a week to help with her homework. Just like Nicola, Giselle had fallen in love with her. Marcelle couldn't deny that she was a sweetheart either. He'd taken a liking to her immediately, and it helped that they were very close in age.

The day of the Dance Pointe recital had finally arrived and Nicola was so ready to show everyone the routine she and Rhianne had been practicing all summer. Once they took their place on the stage, she looked into the audience and saw the rows of seating their family had taken up.

Giselle, Lowell, Marcelle, Patrick, Suzy, and Ms. Mabel were seated just in front of Melanie, Randy, Shanae, and Aunt Lorraine. She made eye contact with her mom, who mouthed, 'kill it baby' just before the DJ started music.

From the first few moves, the audience was hollering something crazy. It was apparent that Miss

Kiara had saved the best performance for last. Nicola and Rhianne set the stage on fire with their precise movements and in-your-face attitude. They both kept smiles on their faces and were obviously in their element.

By the time Chelley sang the last song, 'Took The Night,' both of their families were on their feet. Deafening applause rang through the auditorium and the two dancers stepped forward center stage to accept their applause.

Afterward as all the dancers and their families mingled and indulged in the refreshments, Giselle chatted with Suzy who was very much showing and glowing at that point. As they engaged in conversation, Suzy took a good look at Giselle. "There's something different about you, what is it?"

"What do you mean?" Giselle was very interested in her answer.

"I don't know, it looks like I'm not the only one who's glowing around here," Suzy said with her head cocked to the side.

Giselle turned red and whispered, "Please don't say anything, I haven't told Lowell yet."

Suzy smiled wide and tried not to react too much. "That's great, congratulations. I didn't know you all were trying."

"We weren't, not yet at least. I was on the pill—don't ask!" They both laughed.

"I'm only four weeks along and found out two days ago. I was waiting for after today to tell him."

"Well isn't this the ever growing family," Suzy stated.

"I know," said Giselle. "We truly are blessed."

Epilogue
A short while later...

From the confines of a nondescript sedan, the man silently watched Shanae and her family exit the performance hall.

In sharp contrast to the joyous look on each member's face, the man's bore a distorted scowl to match the furious heat that coursed through his veins. He studied the group intently, especially Shanae who threw her head back and roared with laughter, apparently at a joke the older woman had recited. His hands formed fists and his jaw clenched as he recalled the disruption she'd brought to his life.

Shanae Alexander would feel his wrath if it was the last thing he did.

Retribution would be his.

www.ingramcontent.com/pod-product-compliance
Lightning Source LLC
Chambersburg PA
CBHW070101260626
47160CB00004B/1272